# BLOOD BY MOONLIGHT

## DARK INK TATTOO
### BOOK FOUR

## CASSIE ALEXANDER

# INTRODUCTION & CHARACTER ART

**Angela:** My secret is out, and now both Mark and Jack know that I'm a werewolf. Worse, my abusive ex-boyfriend, the one who made me this way, has escaped from prison and he's after one thing: our son. The Pack is a brutal, criminal motorcycle gang: I don't want that life for Rabbit. Jack says he can protect us, but the Pack is strong and if they catch us, they'll kill me and take Rabbit. But if I'm going down, I'm taking Gray with me.

**Jack:** She's a monster like me, but that doesn't change how I feel about her. I'll do everything I can to save her and her son. When old enemies reappear and my Mistress betrays me, I might have to give up everything to protect them from the Pack. Angela's entrusted me with her son, and I won't let her down.

*A werewolf ready to make her last stand.*
*A vampire who will do anything to protect the innocent from the unholy.*

**Welcome to Dark Ink Tattoo, where needles aren't the only things that bite...**

Dark Ink Tattoo is a scorching paranormal in the vein of Sons of Anarchy, with strong sexual situations and bisexual MCs.

Content warnings can be found on cassiealexander.com.

# CHAPTER ONE
## JACK

"How soon can we get there?" Angela asked, wide-eyed, now that her man Mark and I had made our deal. And *there* was the werewolf-proof, vampire-guarded bunker in the desert my Mistress could provide for them, if they agreed to her terms.

Angela's question echoed in the small room, as I started thinking.

Rosalie would be thrilled to have Mark's money, of course, and the Fleur de Lis's backing—but—my eyes flickered over to Paco, who knew I was a vampire, and so was surely thinking the same thing: *how close was it to dawn?*

It was already late. What if Mark drove a hard bargain? Or worse yet—what if Rosalie whammied him into an easy one? Once he was in the door, who knew what could happen?

And then on top of that, what was the Pack's timeframe?

"Well?" Mark asked, looking at me.

"We're going to Vermillion," I said.

"The strip club downtown?" he asked.

"Yeah." I snatched my knife back off the table and pocketed it. "I'll meet you there—I need to pave the path with some introductions."

"But you made it sound like—" Angela began, worry creeping back.

"It'll be fine. Bring Paco and then leave him in the car, the place itself is safe." I pushed past them for the stairs.

"I've met the owner of Vermillion socially—and I know Vegas," Mark said, putting out his arm to hold Angela back. "Why hasn't he struck me as the bunker-owning type before?"

"He?" I asked, wondering just who Mark thought the owner of Vermillion was. I paused three steps up, thinking fast. "Are you involved in human trafficking?" I asked. His silence answered me. "I didn't think so. Trust me, you don't know the owner like I do," I said, and finished running up the stairs before he could ask anything else.

Paco followed me. "How much of a lead do you need?" he asked quietly when I reached the kitchen.

"Ten or fifteen—thanks," I said, keys in hand, running for my car.

I PULLED into Vermillion's parking lot and took up two spaces near the front, running out and up to the front door, only to be greeted by Tamo again, sitting on a high stool behind the hostess's podium, looking even more monstrous in an impeccably tailored suit.

"Bouncing?" I asked him.

"Why not?" He gave me a wide and evil grin.

I did my best to look non-plussed. "Where's Rosalie?"

"In back. Why?"

"Business," I said, and sidled past. The club's music hit me like a fist; it was late, anyone still here and partying needed its artificial drum to stay awake and spending. I swiveled my head and saw Rosalie parting the small crowd that remained, like a dark wave.

"Tamo said you were here alone?" she said.

"Yeah." I frowned, and looked behind myself, where Tamo had been obscured by a turn in the club's architecture—and for the first time realized the entryway had been converted into a defensible bottleneck after the latest remodel. "Telepathy?" I wouldn't put any creepy power past Rosalie.

"Radio technology. You might have heard of it?" She laughed and then sobered. "Why are you here, Jack?"

"My friend's interested in the bunker option."

"Oh?" Her eyes lit up with the promise of cash. "Well, where are they?"

"On their way here, shortly. I just wanted to set some ground rules with you, first."

"Really?" she said, her tone somehow managing to capture the complete disdain she had for me.

"Yeah. Is there somewhere we can talk?"

Her lips lifted into a smile showing teeth that were, for the moment, human. "Of course."

ROSALIE LED the way back to her private room. I realized it halfway there, far too late to complain, and I didn't want to seem weak besides. But my gait stiffened, my hands curled into fists, and while she walked across her room to lounge in a chair behind her vanity I stood near the door, for all the good it'd do me.

"Jack, please."

"You're the one that told me that being a vampire meant having a long memory." This room was where she'd changed me.

"Are we reminiscing or are we doing business?" She gestured toward her couch. It was black now, presumably part of her remodel, so not even the same couch I remembered. I grit my teeth and sat down on it, for Angela's sake. "So—the Fleur?"

"Yeah."

She clacked her nails on her vanity in excitement. "Tell me more."

"I can't. I don't know everything, yet."

"Then why're you here?"

"Because I want to make sure you play fairly."

"Jack, if I'd wanted a club at every casino in this city I could have one, easily. You're not the only one with contacts—everyone in Vegas walks through my doors eventually."

"Then why don't you?"

"Because what's better than having business arrangements is having someone *owe* you. And finding reasons to have people owe you is harder than you'd think."

I knew all about how Rosalie liked to be owed. "In case they find out your secret. So they won't hurt you—or tell."

"Precisely. So I'll play fair—mostly—never fear." There was a knock at her door. She went to answer it and stepped outside, returning not that long after. "Sorry, club business. Now—about what your friend requires...."

"The bunker—immediately."

She settled herself regally back into her chair. "It won't be ready until tomorrow night."

"Why?"

"Surely you realize this is short notice, Jack. We use it for storage."

"Of what?"

"You don't want to know. But—what're your next steps? This is related to your werewolf problem, right?"

"Yes." I was still reluctant to tell her anything, but Angela herself would be talking to her shortly. My phone buzzed in my pocket—likely Paco telling me they were leaving. "My friend—she's were. As is her boy. And the Pack can track her. What can you do about that?"

Her eyes glazed in thought. "Difficult—but not insurmountable. I have a magician friend who can help. It'll cost more, of course."

"Of course," I snorted.

"But," she said, drawing the word out. "How long will they need to stay there? Hiding them is not the same as fixing their problem. Why does the Pack even want them?"

"I don't know, yet." I wished I'd gotten a few more minutes alone with Angela in Mark's wine cellar. I still hadn't managed to figure out how Bella and her unborn child had fit in. Except maybe.... "The Pack wants what's theirs?" I guessed.

"The boy?" She considered this. "Werewolves are a slow breeding race—and not for lack of trying, I hear. But why on earth would he be special?" Her eyes narrowed. "Who's his father?"

"Gray."

"Their imprisoned packleader?" She leaned back in her chair and cursed.

"She just needs to buy some time—to figure out a plan to get away."

"Time isn't going to fix this—it's a fight for succession, Jack. Legitimate male heirs—ones born, not bitten—are rare."

I rocked back on my heels. "So? If your magician can stop them from being able to trace her, she can go to ground."

"They won't stop looking."

"The world's a big place. Besides—what other choice do they have?"

Rosalie stood and started to pace. "Apart from hiding them, we'll have to have guards, night *and* day. I'll have to pull some of my girls from here, which'll be a loss of income—mine and theirs—and we'll need enough blood slaves to keep our strength up, and they, in turn, will need food. Not to mention that none of the ammunition we have will work, as it's not like I keep silver in stock."

I was taken aback by her use of the word 'blood slaves.' "There are normal people that know?"

"Don't worry your pretty little head about it," she said, dismissively. I made a mental note to come back to the topic the second Angela was safe. "How many days will you need?"

"I don't know."

"Well, the price will rise exponentially, as the risk does. It won't take long for the Pack to realize their beloved leader's bitch has gone to ground."

I grit my teeth. "Don't call her that."

"Temper, temper," she warned, still pacing. I could see her doing the calculations in her head—in her life before this one, whatever time period it'd been in, she must've been an accountant. "What kind of cover story did you give me?"

"I said you were a human trafficker."

At that, she guffawed. "Quite."

"Speaking of—he thinks you're a 'he' for some reason."

"Ahh—he's met one of my friends before is all. You know the difficulties of managing day life—I tell assorted men they own Vermillion, and then they helpfully file my permits with the city during daylight hours."

I snorted. "Gotcha."

"Now," she said, standing straight and raising her chin to a regal height. "Time to see how much we can shake Mr. Carrera down for." She turned on her heel, and headed for the door.

"Wait—they're here?"

"Got here right after you. Been alone out there for, oh, fifteen minutes?" Rosalie saw the haunted expression on my face. "Oh, come now, Jack. What's the worst they could've gotten into?"

# CHAPTER TWO
## ANGELA

As soon as Jack left, Mark made to follow—and Paco tried to stop him.

"Do you work for him or for me?" Mark bellowed.

Paco's expression went steely, but then he glanced at me before answering. "For you," he answered, while subtly making it clear he was on my side.

Why was that? He and Jack had history—and I suspected that he knew about Jack being a vampire, maybe even about Rabbit and me. Safe behind Mark's broad shoulders I nodded quickly, trying to tell him that I, too, was in on Jack's secret.

"Good," Mark said. I could feel him folding his temper up, to tuck it back inside. "You two will stay here—I'll round up some of the other men to drive."

"No," I protested. "I have to come with you."

"Why? That doesn't make any sense, Angie—you should stay here with Rabbit."

"I...." I stalled, trying to come up with a reason he'd believe. "I need to know what I'm getting into. I can't just drag Rabbit into dealing with criminals." The truth was, I couldn't send Mark into a vampire pit, alone. Jack was a good man, but he wouldn't watch out for Mark like I would. I turned to Paco. "If you stay here, will Rabbit be safe?" I trusted him to tell me the truth.

"I'll guard him with my life," Paco said solemnly and I believed him.

"See? Please." I walked forward and interlaced my fingers with Mark's. "Whatever decisions we make—I want to make them together."

At that, Mark relented. "All right. Go get in the car."

"I'll send men down to drive and guard you." Paco reached for his earpiece.

"Thanks," Mark said curtly, and we were both walking for the front door.

ONE OF PACO'S men held the door of a black sedan open for me and I slid into the back while Mark walked around to the far side. Both of the other men—a guard and a driver—sat up front, one of them always looking at the road, the other looking around, swiveling his head or scanning the mirrors.

If the Pack attacked, some of these men might die—for me. It was an uncomfortable feeling, no matter how well they were being paid. It didn't seem to bother Mark though, in the least.

"You're being awfully quiet," he murmured. His hand found mine and covered it entirely.

"It's been a long few days."

"The end's in sight."

*You can't know that,* I wanted to say, but the words died on my tongue. He lived in a world where if you paid enough money, you could guarantee your safety, eventually, it was just a matter of time. Whereas the world I lived in—I looked out the window. The moon was almost full.

"I meant what I said earlier, Mark."

"Which part?"

*All of it—even the 'Rabbit and I are werewolves' part.* But I couldn't say that—or anything about vampires—in front of the other men. "I love you," I said, after too long a pause.

"I love you, too," he said, and reached over to pull me toward him, as far as the seatbelts would allow. I unclicked mine—dying in a car crash seemed the least of my current concerns—and snuggled up against him.

THE DRIVER PULLED us into Vermillion's lot, parking near Jack's car. I could feel Mark weighing whether or not he needed the men to come inside with us, deciding against it.

"Stay here—but if anything happens—or if people rush out—"

"We'll come in."

"Are you sure you don't want to bring at least one of them?" I asked, once both car doors were closed.

"This is a business arrangement, between two business people. I've played poker with the man prior—I don't have any reason to believe that he'll screw me. He just never struck me as someone involved in an underworld organization before."

I crossed around to reach his side, and we were finally alone. "There's something I have to tell you," I said, pulling him to a stop right outside Vermillion's doors. "And it might change your mind about all this, Mark." *Or make you question my sanity.*

"Yeah?"

"The people that work here—the ones that Jack knows...." I left my mouth open, trying to say the words *'are vampires'* with all my might. But nothing came out. What had happened? Jack had told me not to tell, and somehow I couldn't anymore?

"What?" Mark gently prompted.

I closed my mouth. *Oh no, oh no, oh no.* "I just think we should just assume the absolute worst about people, from here on out."

He gave me a half-smile. "I'm a lawyer. I always do," he said, and held his arm out for me to take.

WE WALKED into the club side-by-side. The interior was trying to be classy but not quite succeeding—after having been in Mark's house and in the Fleur, I knew what class truly was.

A broad-shouldered bouncer-type met us after we walked in the door, a little shorter than Mark but he made up for it in width. Was he a vampire, too? I begged my wolf to come out of her silver-induced haze to help protect me. "Welcome to Vermillion—what kind of entertainment were you looking for this evening?"

"I'm here to meet Patrick Bjornson."

The bouncer's eyebrows subtly rose. "Let me see if I can find him for you," and he stepped away, putting a hand to his ear. When he returned, he was all smiles. "Of course—you're expected. He's had a slight delay in leaving his house—can I take you to a meeting room?"

"Please," Mark answered for the both of us and as the bouncer turned we followed him in.

The music was loud and pulsing, and there was no way to not see the gorgeous women lounging and strolling on the floor level, or strutting on the stage as we passed it. A woman came up to us and offered us drinks, *'On the house!,'* and we both took one to be polite, as we passed through an archway, to a quieter area of the club and at last to a doorway, where he gestured us inside.

"We don't have traditional meeting rooms, unfortunately—but there's tables and chairs here," the bouncer explained.

"And a stage, and a pole," Mark said, commenting on the rest of the decor.

The bouncer smiled. "Indeed. I'll be back as soon as Mr. Bjornson arrives."

"Thanks," Mark said, tilting his glass at the man before sitting down at a seat where he had a clear view of the door. I sat beside him, putting my untouched glass down. This was as good a place as any to try to begin to explain.

"So about earlier—when I was being awful," I began.

"When you were stressed and sad," Mark said, reaching over to squeeze my knee.

"I said some crazy things."

"Like we all have, in similar situations."

"Not too many people shout out that they're werewolves, Mark."

He snorted. "I'd forgotten about that."

"No you hadn't—you don't forget anything. You were just willing to write it off was all."

"Like I said, you've been under a lot of stress lately."

"But what if it was true?" I searched inside myself for the place my wolf usually roamed. She was there, just—quiet. Sluggish. Like the silver I'd so rashly drank had turned into shackles, weighing her down. If I couldn't warn him about vampires, I had to warn him about me. "Mark," I said and inhaled, ready to press my case, then the door opened again. I went quiet and Mark stiffened, in anticipation of Mr. Bjornson's arrival—but instead the person who walked through was an astoundingly beautiful woman, wearing a short coat tied around her waist and particularly high heels. She flashed both of us a nervous smile.

"Mr. Bjornson said that I should entertain you until he gets here."

"How kind of him," Mark said, graciously.

She did a combination of a shrug and a curtsey, and then walked over to the stage, hopping onto it ass first, before swinging her legs up onto it so that she could stand. She towered over us from her much higher vantage point, red hair cascading over both of her shoulders, and gave both of us a long look before reaching behind her to find the pole.

Mark and I instantly looked at one another and had a conversation with our glances. It was odd, sure, but nothing about the night had been normal so far—and for all we knew, this strange woman was Mr. Bjornson's personal secretary...or daughter. I shrugged, and

Mark gave me a lopsided grin. There were more worrisome things in both our lives than an attractive woman dancing for us.

Except for the other things I knew. "Mark," I murmured, trying to find words I was allowed to speak. He took my struggle for nervousness, and tossed an arm around me as music came on with a mesmerizing beat. The woman grinned at us, wriggled down the pole, spreading her knees, though the shade from her coat hid what lay inside, and then worked her way back up slowly, the pole at her back. Then she started to circle it lazily, like she was greeting a friend, before grabbing hold of it with both hands to spin around it once, almost half-heartedly, coming down to touch the ground again quickly. She seemed so awkward I almost felt safe—and then she started singing along with lyrics that matched the beat, I could see her lips moving.

*"All eyes on me, me, me, me, me, don't you want to see, see, see, see, see,"* she sang. After that the pole went from being her stiff dance partner to her friend, as she swung herself up high, tossing her legs around almost the top of it to drop her body down. Her hands found the ties of her coat as she spun, and within seconds it was released, revealing skin as white as my own, hidden only by the tiniest of deep purple panties and bikini top.

I heard Mark inhale. I could hardly blame him. The way she moved—she was utterly magnetic. Her hands found the pole between her thighs, pulled herself back up, and then she released her legs, one at a time, in a feat of strength that would've been impossible for me, if I didn't have a wolf inside me. She spread her legs in midair, into a V that pointed towards us and away as she spun, her eyes closed, still whispering the words, her head tossed back—and I realized she wasn't concentrating, she was enjoying this, the pure physicality of her own body.

I...was enjoying it too. Maybe more than I ought to be. I tried to look away—and found I couldn't.

As she wound down the pole, she landed in a gentle seat directly in front of us, the stage putting her legs at a perfect viewing angle—

and she knew it, she folded them in and then crawled over them toward us, green eyes beaming.

"Hey," she said. "I'm Maya."

"I'm Mark," Mark answered—and I found myself able to spare him a glance. His arm was still around me, but his eyes were on her, and between his breathing and the way he leaned forward, I knew he liked what he saw.

So did I. There was something about her—something cat-like—almost alien—and I then realized that she wasn't human.

"Mark!" I said sharply, trying to warn him. But just like I couldn't wake my wolf—I couldn't find the words. I put my hands to my mouth like I could claw out Jack's spell.

*"All eyes on me, me, me,"* Maya whispered, again in time with the song, then she smiled curiously at me and said, *"Shhh,"* putting finger to her lips—and now I was doubly sealed.

Reaching the end of the stage, she swung herself off of it, one long leg at a time before coming over, her hips rolling like a ship in a storm. Her head tilted so all her hair spilled over one shoulder and she stood near, performing a perfect imitation of coquettish innocence, despite the fact that she wore almost no clothing and she was breathing far harder now than she'd been on stage.

"We're all alone in here for a while," she said like that news troubled her, and her lips folded into a tiny pout. "What do you think we should do until they let us out?"

I tried with all my power to say, *Run!*, but nothing came out, even as my terror grew. Where the fuck was Jack? This couldn't have been a set up—

"I have ideas," Mark rumbled from beside me.

"Yeah?" she asked, and stepped closer. *"Tell me."*

He managed to look between us first. "I want to fuck the both of you."

"The loyal type, eh?" she teased, reaching out a hand. Mark took it, and she drew him up, displacing me.

*"Kiss me,"* she demanded, and he did so. I always knew I could be

jealous, in an abstract fashion, but Mark had never given me a reason. But now, seeing him kissing her, watching her lean into him, the way his arms wrapped around her. I mean—I knew he didn't really want her—she'd just told him to want her—*right?*

Then he pulled back and saw me and what must've been my stricken face, and his eyes widened in horror. "Angie," he whispered.

*"It's all right,"* she told him, taking his chin in her hand. "She doesn't mind, does she?"

Mark looked over at me for confirmation. If I told him I did—what would that change here? She could go tell me to stand in a corner and look at a wall, and then I would be blind and I still wouldn't be able to do anything.

What—if anything—was the right thing to do? I didn't know. I shook my head, still mute by her command.

"Good," Maya purred, abandoning Mark and coming over to me. "I wouldn't want you to be lonely."

My lips parted as I struggled to speak, again, with nothing coming out—and her lips sank to meet mine.

I could've—I could've bitten her or something, I suppose—but she was soft and she smelled good and her tongue pushed in gently, as if asking permission, entirely opposite of everything else about her and I kissed her back, leaning in, wondering if my tongue would feel fangs.

"Mmm," she said, when she broke off before me. "You both are delectable." Her heavily lidded eyes took me in. "I want to do such things to you. To both of you," she said, looking over me to Mark. *"Unholster your gun."*

I immediately looked over to Mark—and found him undoing the buckle to a hidden gun-holster I hadn't realized he'd been wearing—I'd been on the other side of him in here and in the car. He placed it on a table behind him, and then looked back to Maya for further instructions.

*"Now unholster your other one,"* she said, giving his crotch a meaningful look, and his hands went for his belt buckle.

Her attention returned to me before I could hide my emotions: shock, horror, jealousy, fear. "Don't worry—I'll make sure he enjoys it. And if you play your cards right, you will too."

At the thought of that, with her, with him, my mind went to unbidden places and heat inside me rose. Goddammit—there was *something*—just being in her *presence*. Could Jack do this when he wanted to? Thank God he'd never done it to me—

And then she was kissing me again, and somehow nothing'd ever felt more right. She pulled back before I was ready to release her, leaving me swooning.

"Every time I touch you, it shocks me." She tapped my lips with her finger as if to prove her point. "It's mystifying."

I had no idea what she was talking about, only vague memories of other people saying the same thing—and then her hand wound around my head and into my hair and pulled me forward again. Then we were kissing and I wanted to put my hands on her. Sensing my hesitation she pulled back and whispered, "Yes. *Do*."

And then it was an imperative. Her skin was so soft, and there was so much of it exposed for me. She made small noises each time my hand lifted and touched, like I was hurting her—and like she enjoyed it.

"Oh, yes." She pulled back from me and then she cast a glance over her shoulder at Mark, who was watching the both of us with his pants half-down and an eager hard-on. "C'mere, loverboy," she said, crooking her finger for him to follow as she pushed me back toward the stage.

We danced together until the stage was at my back, then she reached behind me to tap at it, making it clear that I ought to hop up. I did, and then we were on a level where she wouldn't have to reach down to kiss me again—and as she did so, I felt her move her hand behind her, to where Mark now was, and knew she was taking hold of him, feeling her sway as he thrust into her hand near her back.

She stopped kissing me, twisted back to kiss him, and then looked between us. "*Don't be afraid. You both want to be with me. And I want to be with you,"* she said, quenching any remaining fear. I could feel it pulling away to hide wherever my wolf was, down, down, down inside.

As she leaned back to kiss him again, I brought down the fabric of her bikini top to kiss her breast. Her free hand held me there, fingers curling against my scalp as I sucked on the ruddy pink of her nipple. Mark's hands circled her and found me and started pulling my shirt up, even as she made him moan and—

It was like being with Willa and Gray again, only not—things were tangled—hands, hair, tongues. Watching him kiss her somehow felt right, and I reached behind her to stroke him myself as she reached her hands down to push my skirt up and pull my underwear down. I rocked my hips back and forth to help her, as Mark leaned over her head to kiss me. Without thinking I started to lay back. She purred and ran her hands up underneath my shirt, pushing it up to expose me, shoving my bra out of the way to take my breasts in her hands.

She felt so warm; everything she was doing inspired heat in me —my worries were a distant memory at best. Her touch, her scent, the sounds she made, the way she caught me with her eyes— between her kisses and the way her hands kept trailing all over my body—I wasn't in control anymore. I didn't even remember how to be.

Maya rose up and looked over her shoulder at Mark. "Your girl is lovely."

"I know," Mark murmured, from where he'd been trailing kisses against her back.

She reached up and ran her fingers through his hair. "So which of us do you want to fuck first?"

He answered without hesitation, "Angie."

She looked momentarily peeved—her eyes flashed and her hand on my thigh tightened. "So you're a good boy, eh? Too bad—for this to work, I'm gonna need you to be dirty." She held onto my legs with both hands and arched herself back for him. *"I'm gonna need for you to fuck me good,"* she said, giving him a helpless glance. "It's been so long," she said, dramatically.

I, of course, knew she was lying—but Mark—he reached down and I could see him pushing her panties aside the way he'd so often pushed mine and—I watched his face as she bent over me to take his cock.

That look—I knew that look—eyes half-lidded, strong jaw slightly dropped. I felt her rock over me—rub over me more like—as his cock found itself deep inside her. It was like watching extraordinarily personalized porn on TV.

"Oh!" she protested—for real or show, I wasn't sure—and then his hands grabbed her waist and his hips started pumping. She held herself over me on her elbows—I could feel each of his thrusts ripple through her as her eyes closed. "Yeah—just like that—that's good—that's so good," she breathed, in time with his strokes. Then her eyes opened, and she started kissing me.

I didn't know what to think. Her breasts were against mine—I wrapped one arm around her back and when the other reached for her clit, her head rose up. "You've done this before," she said, and it wasn't a question. "Good." Her hands found my thighs and with her greater strength she pushed me up the stage. *Keep your legs wide for me."*

Without being able to stop myself, my knees fell, one to each side.

"Making him come was always going to be easy," she said, as Mark still rhythmically pulsed in and out of her. One of her arms folded in so that her hand could open my pussy wide. "But making you come," she said, before leaning down to kiss my clit, "is going to be a treat."

After that—her mouth fully found me and there was nothing I could do. She somehow ate me out with both fervor and precision—she always seemed to know exactly what I needed next, when things were too much and she needed to back off, and when I needed more-

more-more, while behind her, Mark fucked her like a machine, making her rock against me in his rhythm.

I didn't know what to do—what I could do? I couldn't even move my hips against her—but there was no way to stop the orgasm building deep inside, no way to deny her what she so clearly wanted—I reached for her head with both hands and grabbed hold of her hair to keep her there, just as she arched further back for Mark and whispered, *"Harder, harder,"* for him and, *"Sing for me,"* to me.

Mark did as he was told, looking over her at me.

"Oh—Angie," he said, like her pussy was mine, just as her tongue flicked back under my hood. My voice returned at last, so I could shout my orgasm out, vibrating with Mark's final thrusts as he shoved himself into her and she translated that movement into me.

She rose up from me then, her lips covered in my juices, her hair in disarray from my hands, looking feral. "Yes," she said, taking the whole moment in with closed eyes. Then her lips drew back and fangs emerged and I knew what she wanted and I couldn't close my legs to run away. I shrieked out my terror and called for the only person who I thought could save me.

"Jack!"

# CHAPTER THREE
## JACK

E ven above the din of the club, I heard Angela call my name. I bolted from the room at the sound, plunging through the crowds of men watching the girls on stage, until I found myself in the room where I'd personally entertained those five women—except now there was quite a different show happening on stage.

I reached Maya's side in a heartbeat and grabbed a fistful of her hair, yanking her back. I smelled sex and cum—but there wasn't any blood, yet. "What do you think you're doing?"

"What do you think you're doing?" she asked back, glaring at me as her fangs receded. She was completely unashamed I'd caught her here, getting fucked and fucking. I couldn't say the same for Angela, who was trying to cover herself up with her skirt, but moving like her back had been snapped.

"Let them go," I growled.

"I would've only taken a little. And then I would've told them to forget."

"Let them go, or I'll take your teeth."

Maya growled back, but made a negating sound, and suddenly

Angela was able to scurry back the way she wanted too. I threw Maya against the opposite wall as Rosalie and Tamo walked in.

"Did you know about this?" I confronted her. Angela rolled off the stage and was rounding on Mark, helping him to pull up his pants like a child.

"No," she said, giving Maya an almost palpable wave of disdain.

"They were handsome, and I was hungry," Maya said.

"I remember you, sparkling one." Rosalie walked over, grabbed Angela's wrist, and let go just as Angela shook her off. "She's laced with silver, Maya. I doubt you would have survived your indiscretion —you're lucky Jack saved you."

"Just what the hell is happening?" Mark asked, finally returning to himself. Angela had gotten his pants zipped and his belt buckled, but his shirt was still untucked, and I was sure his balls felt lighter. He immediately made himself big and tried to control the situation. "Who are you all? Where's Mr. Bjornson?"

"I humbly and deeply apologize for making you wait here," Rosalie said, taking point, pressing an earnest hand to her décolletage and bowing slightly.

"Who the fuck are you?" Mark asked, grabbing Angela, holding her firmly to his side.

"I'm Mistress Rosalie, the owner of this establishment. I believe you recently sampled some of our delights."

Mark's hand around Angela's shoulder tightened. "You—she," he sputtered as his neck spun. Once he'd spotted Maya he wasn't going to let her out of his sight again.

"Go," Rosalie said, and a half-naked Maya ran for the door.

"She tricked us. She used me," Mark started explaining, both to himself and to Angela.

"I know, baby, I know," she crooned. "It's okay, we need to leave this place, all right? Whatever they've got—it's not worth it." She gave me a look over her shoulder that broke my heart.

"Come now," Rosalie said, placing herself between them and the door. "Something tells me you enjoyed it. The both of you. Even if you don't fully understand why."

"We're leaving," Mark announced, and grabbed Angela so firmly it was clear he'd carry her out the door if he had to.

"What happened to you is why they can protect her," I said. It was also the only excuse for why I'd brought her here.

"Indeed." Rosalie made a gesture, and Tamo brought her a chair, in which she sat down. "You can go and forget this night ever happened, counting down the moments until the Pack regains your girl—or you can listen to my terms."

"Which are?" Mark asked archly.

"We're vampires, dear boy. And your girl—while she's not one of us, we are akin."

Mark's eyebrows rose high, as he swiveled his head to include me. "Vampires? Please."

"*Stand straight. Let go of the girl.*" Rosalie said and Mark hopped to. "Do jumping jacks. Go fuck a tree," she said with less conviction and he reached for Angela again. "I could make you dance like a marionette, but that's not why either of us are here. Your girl needs protection from her werewolf ex-boyfriend, and I want access to the Fleur De Lis."

Angela's jaw dropped, as Mark twisted to look at her.

"You hadn't told him yet?" Rosalie guessed.

"I'd been trying," she said, to Mark. "I'm so sorry, Mark—I tried, you know I did."

Rosalie clucked. "Well he'd best listen to me, because we've got about four hours left to hammer out a contract if we're going to. Are we?"

I studied Mark. I'd been jealous of him for so long, this man who was seemingly the answer to all of Angela's prayers, who could provide for her in so many ways I couldn't—which way would he cut now that the cards were on the table?

It was like a mask of steel replaced his face as he next spoke to Rosalie. "Go on."

MARK WAS NOT ONLY A LAWYER, but a lawyer's lawyer. They all sat around a table, Rosalie, Tamo, Angela, Mark; pen and paper were brought out. Square footages and percentages were discussed until agreed upon, as were the terms of Angela and Rabbit's safety. I hung out against the wall, listening, watching Angela react. Mark seemed to have taken the news of her being a werewolf well, but she was still nervous, I caught her picking at her hem. She glanced up and noticed me noticing, gave me a look that was difficult to read, and stopped.

They seemed to be in accordance when Mark flipped the paper over to reveal an empty page which he quickly filled with bullet points before presenting it to Rosalie—and when she read it, she recoiled.

"You're joking."

"It's the only way I'll sign it." He twisted in his seat to see me. "Come here, Jack." I stepped forward and he shoved the paper into my hands. "I trust you—I think. Or I trust that you love Angela enough to not let anything bad happen, at least."

I had the unfamiliar sensation of blood rising to my cheeks, and glanced over at Angela, as she looked away. "Yeah."

"So read it. Is it solid?"

Angela was still looking elsewhere. I'd been a fool to bring her here and put her in so much danger—my gaze slowly fell to the sheet of paper I held. On it, Mark had done an amazing job of cornering Rosalie. All the arrangements they were making tonight were final, neither one of them could ever change a thing—which was to say that she couldn't control Mark into changing his mind later—and that if something happened to him, the contract immediately became null and void, and whatever business enterprise Rosalie had built within the Fleur would—quite literally, according to the terms he'd set—have to be destroyed. Rosalie would get everything she wanted—but keeping it would depend on Mark still breathing.

I nodded to Mark and handed it back, but Angela intercepted it, reading it quickly. "All this—for a week?"

"Mostly just the next forty-eight hours," Rosalie said. "Getting you and your son's trails cleared will be the biggest hurdle. My magician will be ready by eleven tomorrow night—I'll send him over—and then after that, we'll transport you to my bunker. Past that, your man here will have to figure how to get you safely out again."

"Where will we go? What will we do?" Angela asked, turning towards Mark. He still had his mask of steel on.

"First, we need to finalize our contract."

Which is how—a few hours later—I learned that in addition to having all night tattoo parlors, Vegas also had all night notaries.

# CHAPTER FOUR
## ANGELA

Mark and I drove back to his place in silence in the backseat of the sedan, each of us firmly on our separate sides. When we got out, Paco greeted us at the door and assured me Rabbit was safe, but that didn't stop me from running upstairs to make sure. I found him curled up into a peaceful ball on his bed, and I sat down beside him, watching him snuggle tighter.

*Tonight, oh my God, tonight.* The last bead on a long necklace, strung with insanity. I watched Rabbit's chest rise and fall with each of his sweet breaths. Everything I'd done, I'd done for him, and he didn't know it. How much longer could I protect him from the truth?

And thinking of people who I couldn't protect anymore—I swept up to standing, and walked back down the hall.

By the time I came down, Mark was ensconced behind his bar. "Drink?" he asked, and started making me one without waiting for my answer.

I kicked off my shoes and stepped down into his living room, feeling the plush gray-green carpet against my feet like silvered moss. "I tried to tell you. Honestly."

"Uh huh," he said, concentrating on his stirring. "How long have you known?"

"That I'm a werewolf? Ever since I was pregnant with Rabbit."

"And Jack?" He handed a drink out to me, and I took it only to set it back down.

"Wine cellar. Earlier tonight. I didn't know vampires were a thing before that—although I probably should've guessed."

He took a long sip of his drink, and I had a feeling it was something stiff. "Did you know it was going to be like that?"

"No. If I had, I never would've allowed it."

He nodded, and set his drink down. "That...was expensive."

"I'm sorry. You were willing to kill a man for me. I assumed that money would be less bothersome. But—I had no idea."

"Me either," he said, a little too forcefully. I didn't lower my gaze —I just took my drink and walked over to the couch.

If he wanted to yell and rail against me now was the time—and as he started to pace back and forth in the room, all I could think was, *Here it comes.*

He finally brought himself to a standstill in front of me. "I won't believe it until you show me."

"Why not?"

"Because—otherwise it sounds insane."

"Like having a three-way with a woman neither of us knew? Wait, that sounds totally like us." I slumped back, took a long sip of something warm and amber, and tucked my legs up. "What about like having a woman order you to unholster a gun—that I didn't know you were carrying by the way—and you just doing it on her command?"

"Yeah."

"And the part where," I pointed to my mouth with two fingers. From his vantage point behind her, had he been able to see her teeth?

"And the mind control bullshit. The way I wanted to be with her, even when I knew I wanted you." He ran his free hand through his hair. "All of that aside though—I still want to see."

I took a moment to search through myself, like I was rummaging through memories. My wolf was ignoring me. "I can't."

"You won't? After all we've gone through tonight?"

I shook my head quickly. "No, Mark. I don't know *how*. I've never let her out before—and after my mom died—I drank her away."

His brow furrowed in confusion. "Your mother?"

"No, my *wolf*. There was so much blood at my apartment—I was so mad—my wolf wanted out, to protect me—and I burned her down." I got a flash of my wolf again—with a jagged streak of furless skin from ear to muzzle-tip, and knew that I had done that to her. Would it grow back? "Here—wait."

I ran upstairs, grabbed my vial of silver, and returned. "See? It's colloidal silver. I drink a little every day, to keep her in check."

He took the bottle from me, uncapped it, and smelled. "This?"

"Yeah. I give Rabbit some, too. I don't know what else I can show you." I'd built an entire life around not having any proof.

For a second I was worried he was going to add it to his drink. But then he closed the bottle and set it down on the bar, like a new mixer. "Can you do it to me?"

It took a moment for me to parse what he was asking. "Change you?"

"Yeah," he said, nodding with determination. "If I were like Gray, I could fight him."

"No. Gray's a wolf through and through. I don't think anyone bitten in would have a chance. Besides," I said, plucking at the skirt I wore, "I wouldn't wish this on anybody."

Mark leaned back against his bar, setting his elbows on it behind him. "Where is this going, Angie?"

"We break the connection between me and Rabbit and the Pack, we breathe for a few days, and then we keep going."

"I can't just leave here. Vegas is my entire life."

"I wasn't really asking you to come with me," I said quietly. There it was. The words I'd been trying to say for so long. Mark looked stunned.

"But—I love you."

"And I love you." I set my drink down and raked my hands through my hair. "But I've been trying to put my foot down with you for weeks, Mark, and you kept not letting me. You always think that you know what's best—"

"I didn't sign all those contracts tonight to lose you, Angela."

"And I didn't let you sign all those contracts so that you could die!" I picked up my drink, slammed it back, and set it down. "I'm sorry—I'm sure it seems like I've been using you—but what it really was, was hope, Mark. Hope that someday we'd come across a solution. You murdering Gray seemed like it was going to work, it really did. But now that my mom's died, and the Pack is clearly planning something—I can't lose you, too. I couldn't bear it."

His eyes narrowed and his wide jaw clenched. "You don't get to decide that for me."

I gave a tiny nod. "Yeah, I do."

He started to pace again, this time in circles. "I can close up shop. There's other places—the family will understand."

"There's nowhere on earth like Vegas, Mark. And you—you belong here. It's your home."

"You don't get to tell me where I belong. I know where I belong," he said, thumping his chest with one hand. "I belong beside you. No matter where you run off to."

I was so tired of crying and yet I couldn't help myself. This was it, we were through. "You can't be beside me anymore, Mark." I said it so quietly it was hard to hear—but if I listened closely I thought I could hear his heart breaking—or maybe it was just mine.

He didn't say anything, and he waited so long I was afraid that that was it, that we were finished—the moment I'd both longed for and dreaded, finally come to pass.

"Angela, please. Just—one last time," he whispered.

And like some kind of fool, I ran across the room to land in his arms.

WHAT FOLLOWED WAS A FUCKING of desperation, on both sides. We kissed until our lips swelled and bruised, our hands sought out every piece of skin, and our clothes might as well have been ripped off of both of us. I wound a leg around him and he used it to pick me up, holding me bodily to him, and I reached down between us to help his cock slide in.

Mark grunted as he landed deep. I reached my other leg up and kept my arms wrapped around his neck, his mouth at my throat. Both his hands were on my ass, holding me up and he bounced me as he thrust, grunting again. Whatever he wanted, however he needed this to be—he wanted to use me, and I wanted to be used.

He paused, looking around, and I knew he was searching for a suitable location for fucking. Without consulting me he picked me up and off of him, and then spun us both around, turning me to face the bar.

I knew what he wanted without asking. I lay down on it, ass up, only the tips of my toes managing to touch the ground, and he growled low as he entered me again. His hands ran up my body and then took hold of the bar's far edge, using it to propel himself even deeper inside of me.

"Oh God," I whispered, feeling myself spread wide and him slide so deep—the edge of the bar cut into my thighs, and my breasts were cold against its metal surface, but I didn't care. One of his hands wrapped into my hair, yanking my head back for him.

"It doesn't matter where you go, what you do, who you do," he said, punctuating himself with long thrusts, "No one else is ever going to love you like me, Angie."

I had a feeling that was true—that it'd been true for the entirety of our relationship. Mark's love was like he was, big and strong and bright, and each time he pushed in me my pussy wanted to grab around him and never let him go.

And me? I wanted him to love me this last time in every place I had. I let go of the bar's edge and, reaching back, spread open my ass.

It took him a second to realize what was being offered—and then I heard him make a guttural, animalistic, response. He rode my pussy hard for three more strokes, and then pulled out slowly, languorously, leaving me aching inside. Then he let go of my hair to take hold of his cock and play its wet head against my tightness.

I shivered, missing what I'd had, nervous about what was to come, as I felt him press in, ever so slightly while I tried to relax. He teased me there, with greater control than I would have had, bobbing the head of his cock in and out, deliciously stretching me until I wanted more.

"This?" he asked, politely from behind. I nodded against the bar's cool metal—and gasped as he finally pushed in.

It...took a while. I'd never been stretched quite like that before. But the tension of him restraining himself to not hurt me, plus the way that it felt as I got more and more of him inside—I slid a hand between my legs without thinking to rub at my clit just as he started his final slide.

"Oh God, Angela," he said, using my thighs for purchase this time, pulling me against him, as his cock went deep and he held it in me. "Your ass feels amazing—I should've been fucking it all along."

The way he was making me feel—I should've let him. I arched into him as much as I could in answer and brought my other hand underneath me, to hold myself up on my forearm, letting the cold metal of the bar lap at my breasts, as I was moved by his thrusts.

"It's good, right?" he asked me, with a note of concern. I'd been quiet because I didn't want to give him hope—but I didn't want him to doubt me, either.

"It's so good, Mark—so good," I said, earnestly, and let myself start to moan.

After that, we didn't need words. Just the slick sound of him thrusting, the damp slap of his balls against my dripping pussy and fingers, each satisfied grunt he made as he went in, the long quiet moans I made as he pulled out, and a tiny metallic swaying from a series of barware that's base must've been bolted down.

Neither one of us wanted to come—if we did, this was over, all the way—but our bodies had other plans. His balls hit my fingers just so, as he pulled out and then landed back in, and the rhythm of that added to what my body was already unconsciously doing, rubbing and stroking my clit. And as for him, I could feel him start to speed up without meaning to, needing more of me, more from me, as my ass began to clench—my toes kicked, looking for purchase, wanting to send myself even higher for him as he plunged down, hands on my shoulders now, riding me hard, his grunts giving way to growls giving way to snarls—I felt his cock stiffen straight inside me, I knew he was close, and knowing that—made me come.

"Mark!" I cried out his name while writhing, feeling my ass grasp him tight as all of me spasmed, grinding my ass against him.

"Oh yes—Angie, yes," I felt him rear back and shove his cock deep for me to take, and then felt him stroke in and out of my tightness, filling me with his load. "Yes," he said again, still thrusting, hips twitching back and forth, and I knew if I'd reached my hand down I could've felt his balls tighten as they finished pouring into me. "God, yes," he said, and then leaned over me, still inside me, kissing my neck, my shoulders, my back.

I could've reached back and kissed him then. We'd fucked all night before, my man was insatiable, it would've been nothing to move to the couch and wait for round two. But that wouldn't have been right—*right?* I pressed myself up onto my elbows instead, waiting for him to move.

He put his hands on either side of me and slid his cock out slowly, making both of us hiss. We both waited, panting, and he broke the silence first. "I can't believe I'm never going to get to fuck you again."

I swallowed and turned around as he made room for me. "I will never, ever, forget this, Mark."

A sad smile fluttered across his face. "You'd better not. And...if you want to come back someday, you'll know where to find me."

I nodded and gave him my own sad smile in return. He stood. He wanted to kiss me, I could feel it, but he knew if he did I might pull away and ruin this memory. So instead he stooped to gather up all of his articles of clothing, giving me one last look before walking up the stairs. "Good night, Angela."

"Good night, Mark," I said. I waited for five minutes to firm my resolve before doing the same, but turning the other direction at the top of the stairs. I took a shower, pulled on boxers and a t-shirt, and went to sleep beside Rabbit, for whatever good it would do if the Pack attacked.

# CHAPTER FIVE
## JACK

I t was almost dawn again before I reached my apartment complex—and for better or worse, Zach wasn't loitering outside.

I'd had a plan brewing ever since I'd spoken to Rosalie—and luckily everything else that had happened tonight hadn't made me forget it. Christ, what the hell had Maya been thinking? Clearly she hadn't been.

Anyhow—my plan would require blood, and seeing as I'd already turned down Paco's with good reason, I didn't have many other options. I texted Fran while I was still in my car, but doubted she'd come through.

Which left Zach. Zach had told me where he lived, right? Even if he hadn't, I could scent him down—I spent my time before dawn writing a hopefully quirky-yet-confident note—went to his apartment, and slid it under the door, then returned to my own to go to sleep.

When I woke, I had a text from Fran saying, *Sorry, darling,* with a series of frowning faces, which meant I had about thirty minutes to prepare for option two. I showered, I brushed my teeth, pulled back what hair would reach into a small knot at the back of my head instead of using pomade to slick it back, and then I put on everything black I owned, to wait for the doorbell to ring.

At six-thirty-two—and after two whole minutes of doubt—Zach was standing, also freshly showered and shaved, outside. I opened the door, and said, "I *vant* to suck your blood," with an improbable accent, and grinned at him. "Want a drink?"

He laughed nervously, but still came in. "Yeah."

"Beer?" I threaded around him, into my kitchen.

"Sure. I'm not picky," he said, returning to the couch, the scene of yesterday's crime. I met him there, offering him a bottle. "So... vampire roleplaying? Really?"

He'd read my note, probably when he'd gotten home in the morning, and had had all day to consider it.

I gave him a winning smile. "You saw the coffin in my bedroom. It's a strange lifestyle choice—but this *is* Vegas."

"Don't get me wrong," he said. "Yesterday was hot and all—"

"And I bet it's all you thought about today," I interrupted. I knew I was right from the way his blood rose.

"Yeah, it was." He gave a shallow nod. "It's just that—I'm not really a role-play kinda guy."

"Why not? You don't seem to suffer from a lack of imagination."

He gave an awkward shrug. "I just don't want to get hung up in the moment—I don't want to do the wrong thing."

"Zach, I'm going to be the one roleplaying here," I said, gesturing to myself with my beer. "You're just going to be a hapless victim who gets bitten. It won't be that hard."

He pondered this. "Can I fight back?"

"If you want. But only if we have a safeword, obviously. Still like 'dangerous?'"

"Yeah." He stared into his beer for answers, and ran a fingertip around the lip of the bottle, and it was hard not to imagine him doing the same thing with a spit-covered finger to the head of my cock. "Is it going to hurt when you bite me?"

"Not unless you want it to. Do you?"

"I don't know." He bit his lip, then suddenly looked over at me. "Will it make you come?"

"Definitely." I was already getting stiff just thinking about it—about him. "So hard."

He shuddered a little, hearing the promise in my voice, and I heard him swallow. "So what's the set up here?"

"It's night, and I've lured you home with the hope of an intense fucking." I gave him a wolfish grin. "Kind of like right now."

He snorted, then set his beer down. "I wish it weren't raining so hard outside," he said, after a long pause.

It was Vegas, there wasn't a cloud in the sky—he'd just decided to try to play with me. It was hard not to bud fangs in anticipation. I stood, moved back to my computer to find a loop online of lightning and rain and played it at a high enough volume so the neighbors wouldn't hear us. "I know. When I found you, you were soaked," I said, dimming all the lights as I returned to him, imagining him with a wet t-shirt on. "And the radio says there's flash flood warnings on all the roads."

"If you hadn't picked me up, I'd still be out there, hitch-hiking."

And here he thought he wouldn't get into it. "Yeah—you're not getting to LA tonight, I'm afraid."

"I guess my audition will just have to wait," he said, with a sly grin that belayed his innocent tone. "So...it's okay if I stay?"

"Yeah. Until morning."

"Good." His hands went for the bottom of his t-shirt and started pulling it up to reveal tanned skin. When he freed himself from it and tossed it aside, I spoke without thinking.

"Has anyone ever told you you're beautiful?"

Zach looked taken aback—not knowing if I was in character, or not. "No."

And then it was my turn to wonder if it was Zach answering for himself, or for Zach-the-imaginary-hitch-hiker. "That's too bad—because you are." I stood, and decided to go back into character myself. "Let me get you some blankets."

I returned with a stack of them, which he took from me, setting them down beside him on the couch. "Thanks. I was chilly."

"I could get you a dry shirt," I offered, even though we were pretending.

"Do you really want that?" he asked, breaking character.

"No, I just like being difficult." It was too much in my nature. Somehow, pretending had put a wall between us, like a semi-permeable membrane. It made me want to reach a hand out, to test its tension.

Zach took the topmost blanket and held it to his chest. "If you really were a vampire, Jack, what would you do?"

"I would say put that blanket down, please," I said, and he set it aside. I moved to stand in front of him, scooting my coffee table out of the way. "And I would say there's a price for spending the night." I moved down to my knees in front of him, placing my body in between his legs. I took his shoes off, and then his socks, while he watched me, and then I reached for the buckle of his belt. "No one gets anything for free in Vegas, Zach. That's only what the commercials want you to believe." I slid my hand down and felt his hard-on beneath the denim on the inside of his thigh. After opening his fly I grabbed both sides of it and tugged, skidding his hips against the couch toward me as he gasped.

"I didn't know when you picked me up this was what you wanted," he said in quick protest, looking down.

"Let me show you what I want," I growled, and reached into his jeans to pull him out.

His cock fit perfectly into my mouth. The head of it was softly ridged, the sensitive part underneath slightly rough against my tongue and his hands were in my hair, knocking it out of the tie in an instant.

"Oh God, Jack," he breathed, his hips thrusting up. "Oh God, vampire-Jack I mean."

I lifted my head while I kept stroking his shaft. "Maybe I don't just want to suck your blood. Maybe I want to suck all your cum out of you."

"I would let you. Let's take all night," he said, then started moaning—I'd reached in to massage his balls with my free hand, and rising up on my knees I pushed that hand underneath him, to rub at the spot between his balls and his ass. "Jack," he gasped. "Condom—going to—" he warned.

I pulled back only far enough to whisper, "I want to taste you," before sucking his cock back down.

He shivered bodily, all of him winding up, I could feel his ass shake and thighs quiver, the way his balls tightened and his cock twitched, the head of him bobbing at the back of my throat like the end of a tugged fishing pole. He wound his fingers into my hair, pulling my lips taut around his hilt until he released himself with a shuddering sigh, pounding my mouth as his hands pushed my head down, his hot cum jetting out, all over my tongue.

"Fuck, yes," he whispered to himself, as I finished sucking him off, taking every drop of cum with me. Ripples of *life* emanated out from him, fast and shallow. I pulled up and off of him slowly, letting his softening cock slide out, but kept my hand where it was, my middle finger near his asshole. I crept my hand higher and began to play with it.

"You're not going to get off that easy, stranger," I said, gently pushing its tip inside.

"No one's ever done that before," he protested with feigned innocence, while squirming, though we both knew that I'd been in there yesterday.

"When your car broke down outside, was there another house in sight?" I rose up onto my knees to get a better angle beneath him, sliding my finger further in.

He shook his head in pretend helplessness, and the music I'd queued up chose just them to rattle with thunder.

"Then I don't think you have a choice," I said ominously, starting to circle that finger around. His eyes narrowed as his asshole stretched for me. "You're at my mercy now, stranger, and I'm going to keep working on you until you beg me for my cock." His jaw dropped, his breath quickened and his blood rushed. I pulled my finger out of him and took my hand back. "Finish taking off your jeans for me."

He rocked back and forth to shimmy out of them, kicking them away. When he sat back down I used the opportunity to hold his cock and balls and move them to one side, licking the crease between them and his legs.

"Oh my God—how do you know?" he panted.

"I'm a vampire," I said, and pretended to bite his thigh. My fangs wanted out though, his blood was so close now, and singing so strongly. "I'm good at everything," I promised him. "Stand up and turn around." I released him and he did as he was told. I cupped both his muscular ass cheeks in my hands. "Bend over for me, Zach."

He looked back and down at me, before taking hold of the back of the couch. I took his taut buttocks and spread them wide, revealing the asshole inside—I leaned forward and kissed it, pressing against it with my tongue.

His breath changed into sharp gasps. "No one's ever done this to me before," he protested. Was that real or fake? Did it matter? I pushed my tongue against his rim until I fit its tip inside. "Oh, oh," he started, and didn't stop. The tormented sounds he made were music to my ears. His hips rocked, begging me to go deeper, and I rocked back, pushing my thumbs in to take my tongue's place, gently stretching him.

"What is it that you want, stranger?"

The way his hips were throbbing and his breath was catching, I knew exactly what he wanted—I only wanted to hear him say it. "Don't call me stranger, Jack—just, fuck me, please."

"As long as I get my bite."

"Yes—anything," he panted. He would've sold me his grand-mother if I'd asked. As it was—I took my hands away from him and stood, making sure he could hear me getting undressed, my boots scuffing, my belt buckle's clank as I opened it, then its thump as it hit the floor, and the noise of my zipper opening up, then the crinkle of a condom wrapper.

"Is this what you wanted?" I played the head of my condomed cock down the cleft of his ass, where my spit had left him wet for me.

"Please," he begged me.

"Just because you're not a stranger anymore doesn't mean I'll go easy," I warned, set myself, took his hips, and pushed myself in—he took me eagerly, hot and tight. "Your ass was made for this." I leaned over his back so I could whisper in his ear. "Made for me." He moaned as I went on. "Take your cock with your other hand and stroke it."

"But," he began.

"Do as I say." It was hard not to let a hint of the whammy through. I knew he wanted to give away control—and I wanted to take it. One hand obediently sank between his legs, as I put one foot on my couch to go more deeply. He groaned as I stretched him wide, and started pulling at himself.

I crouched over him, kissing his back and neck—I could only reach his lips when I was hilt deep inside of him, catching his head with one hand, twisting him to me. Our hips moved as one as our tongues twined and the way we were panting fell into synch. I broke off first. "I want to come for you, Zach. I want to push you to the edge, and make you take me over."

We were rocking, so tight and hard, thunder crashing around us, the only glow my distant computer screen.

"Tell me when you're ready—when you can't hold it anymore—that's when I want to bite you." I reached around and beneath him, taking control of his cock while he went back to holding onto the couch with both hands, bracing as he moaned. I could feel him tensing again, his body winding up, his ass starting to grab as his cock stiffened.

"Jack!" he warned. "Bite me!"

I waited until the last possible moment as he lost himself, his cum slippery in my hand. I shoved my cock up inside him, pulsing, as my fangs ripped down and I bit him.

Hard, but not savagely.

The shout of his orgasm became a strangled scream—I couldn't always stop it from hurting—and blood, glorious blood welled out. I didn't waste a drop. My fangs receded and I milked the holes I had made with my lips and tongue while my hard cock still speared him and the last of his load leaked out. He cried out again, gasping, but stock still in the manner of prey.

I rose up behind him, feeling *full* in a way I hadn't since I'd last bled Paco, feeling dual waves of life and blood hitting me hard. I slid out of him, panting, tossing the condom aside, and he fell down to my couch, clamping his hand to his neck, with a stunned look in his eyes, verging on hurt, as he opened his mouth to say something.

"Sorry, Zach," I cut him off. "*Forget.*"

Whatever questions he'd been about to ask were erased, even as the wounds I'd made on his neck sealed up. He was still out of breath —but he was young. He wouldn't even realize he was a pint low. "Christ—Jack—fucking you is like doing whippets."

I reached down for my jeans. "Yeah? How so?"

"I feel high and I can't remember the last three minutes."

I grinned at him, jumping my jeans up. "That's a shame. They were pretty good."

"Did—you?" he asked, suddenly concerned.

He wanted to please me. I found it charming. "Oh yeah. You could drown a small child in the condom I tossed."

"Eww," he said and snickered.

"You asked."

"I—I wish I remembered. I remember blowing my load in your mouth though—Jesus, that was hot," he told himself as I walked into my bedroom.

I returned with a clean shirt and then used my old one to swipe up the mess on my couch. "You got a little over excited. Don't worry. You'll get another chance." I leaned in and kissed him.

"Yeah?" he asked, the very image of hope.

"Yeah," I agreed. "But—I'm going on a trip tonight." At which point in time Sugar chose to meow from the kitchen—where she'd gone to hide once the 'thunder' started up. I turned off my computer and returned to Zach. "Hey—I know this is sudden—but can you feed my cat while I'm gone?"

He blinked, the fog my whammy had put around him finally fading. "Uh, sure? But how long will you be?"

"Don't know."

"You don't know?" He sounded incredulous.

I leered at him. "I'm dark and mysterious, Zach."

He laughed. "Like a vampire?"

I gave him a toothy smile. "Precisely."

IT TOOK another twenty minutes to get him out the door—I told him I'd put my house key under the mat for him—and then I rushed to wash my face and brush my teeth again. No time for a full shower, despite the fact that I knew Angela would smell Zach on me—I needed to make a detour before seeing her again.

My car wound its way back to Bella's house like it was pulled there, and I wondered if it was, as if the blood I'd taken from Zach had somehow known why I had needed it.

Not that that changed how I got it, of course. My hand wrung the steering wheel at the thought. I'd *practically* gotten true consent from him, but that wasn't the same as *actual* consent, and I knew that the ethical hair I was splitting was fine. I parked a few houses down from Bella's place again—I'd feel bad about whammying Zach later, when I had time.

Now that it'd been a few days since Bella's murder, I felt safer about breaking back in—and so had other people, apparently. We were a little far from the Strip for squatters, and this neighborhood was too nice for anyone to steal copper—my bet was on bored teens.

Whoever they were, their interest in Bella's things had left her home in even more disarray than the murder had—the crystal skulls were gone now, probably being retrofitted into crystal bongs. Her clothing had been pulled out and strewn across the floor, same for her shoes and purses, the best of all of them stolen, I imagined.

Despite the chaos and the desecration I could still feel her here, riding the high Zach's blood had given me. I sat down in her bedroom in the dark, reaching a hand out to touch her bloodstain.

"I need to know a little more, Bella. I know who did this—and I think why—but I need an angle."

I had a feeling like the pressure changed, like when they seal you up on a plane and your ears start to pop. Bella had been fond of all sorts of magic, and had appropriated from other cultures shame-lessly—which was why the feathers on both a dreamcatcher and an African drum started to sway. My eyes traveled the room in the half-dark, looking for what she wanted me to find—and saw a necklace, looped over the top of her bedside lamp, with its pendant shim-mying in the breeze. I knew what it was. I stood, walked over, and unlooped it, taking its pendant in my hand, even though it burned me lightly. It was a silver planchette—the kind you used on Ouija boards.

The first night I'd met Bella, she'd brought me back here and she'd made me play. The questions she asked seemed so pointless, and of course I assumed she was the one moving the planchette. It wasn't until I'd taken the damned thing and put it in my mouth, holding it between my teeth, and told her that the spirits wanted me to use it to draw on her naked that she laughed, and then agreed. She'd stripped herself naked to lie on her living room floor, where I traced the planchette's sharp point over her soft skin carefully, all the while my mouth burned.

Now that I held its chain, it swung from the far end, tugging me, like I was dowsing with it.

"All right," I said, and went where it pulled me. It took me into her hall closet, behind her water heater, where I found stacks of books hidden, as yet undisturbed. I pulled out a few and found volu-minous notes—strange words I didn't recognize, alongside propor-tions in teaspoons and ounces that I did. All of the books were like recipes. The planchette tugged me to reach over these, and pull out a square of red velvet, in which I found the Ouija game itself wrapped up, tucked beneath a bundle of sage.

I pulled it out and closed the closet door, then went to kneel in her living room, using the moonlight filtering in through her blinds for light. I opened the board and unstrung the planchette, setting it down in the center.

"Bella?" I asked. Nothing. Even the sensation of pressure had subsided. "Dammit." I reached out for the marker and—as my fingers touched one side it spun off like I'd shoved it, to hover over *'Yes.'* Good.

"You were pregnant," I began, and the planchette spun around the word *'Yes'* like a bee doing a dance. "I already know who murdered you—and I promise they will pay." At that the planchette went up on its nose, as if it wanted to pierce through the board. "But I need to know whose baby it was, first."

The planchette fell, then teetered back and forth like an indeci-sive coin, before zooming off on a path. I read the letters quickly. "Jonah?" and it went back to *'Yes.'*

I'd only heard his name once—from the prostitute I'd slept with, Amber, saying he was one of the big dogs of the Pack, so to speak. And as of yet, he wasn't involved in anything with Angela, that I knew of.

"Did he know?"

The planchette crept across the board to *'No.'* Whether the planchette was moving more slowly because Bella was sad for him, or ashamed she hadn't told him, I couldn't say.

It was, however, a start. Gray had been in prison a long time. Surely there were some members of his pack who'd grown used to his absence—and who wanted him to stay in there.

"Did you love him?"

*Yes.*

"Did he love you?"

*Yes.*

If she had the true love of a werewolf—why had she run from the Pack? As if reading my mind, the planchette began tapping more letters in quick succession. *Dark clouds—bad cards—not safe.*

So she'd run—for all the good it'd done her. I rocked back on my heels. "Thank you, Bella."

The planchette wove back and forth like it was waving good-bye —and then it raced out three more words. I knew what she was spelling by the end of the first one.

*Should have stayed.*

"I know," I whispered.

I reached for it before it could cause me anymore grief, and then strung it back on its chain as I stood. I meant to return it, but it wouldn't hurt to have a stinging reminder of my biggest mistake close at hand. I looped the chain around my neck and dropped the planchette beneath the fabric of my shirt, so that I could feel it burn me.

I deserved it.

# CHAPTER SIX
## ANGELA

R abbit and I both woke up late the next day and Mark was gone. I couldn't blame him, I'd dragged his business down long enough, I was sure he had a lot to catch up on—especially after last night. Would the powers that be at the Fleur actually let him wheel and deal on their behalf? Would he still want to, knowing that he couldn't have me?

Rabbit sat on a barstool in the kitchen, kicking his legs against what was no doubt some endangered Brazilian hardwood, hunched over so far on his elbow his face was almost in his cereal milk.

"I can't stop thinking about Grandma."

"I know, baby," I said, sitting beside him, stroking his back. I hadn't bothered with the pretense of food.

"Like why'd they do that, Mom? Why would anyone want to hurt her?"

"They weren't after her, Rabbit. They were after us."

He swiveled his head to look at me. "Why?"

"Because." I'd never told Rabbit anything about his father, ever—but I owed it to him now. If anything happened to me—if Gray did steal him away—he'd never hear the truth until it was too late. I reached out for his hands and he gave them to me, along with his full concentration.

"You know how I always told you your father died?"

His eyes widened and he nodded.

"He's not dead. He's been in prison this whole time. He killed a woman—he killed lots of women."

I held his hands tighter as I watched the news rock him.

"But—why—why'd you lie? Why didn't you ever tell me?"

"Because he's a bad man, Rabbit. Some of his friends are the ones that killed Grandma."

"Why?" he asked, his volume rising.

If I told him 'they were looking for you' he might feel responsible, and that wasn't fair. My boy was only seven, almost eight, he shouldn't have to carry that kind of burden.

"They were after us. Because they're bad. They just wanted to hurt us, was all."

His face was red, fresh tears started streaming from his eyes, and his lips peeled back as he tried to speak instead of sob. "Well it worked!" he shouted. I let go of his hands, and took him into my arms.

"I know, baby. I'm so, so sorry. I wanted to tell you earlier—but I was scared."

"They—they took Grandma," he said, shuddering into me.

"I know," I said, rocking him. Mark appeared in the doorway across from us. He was dressed in a suit, but he looked worse for the wear. He jerked his head slightly, asking if he could talk to me, and I nodded, mouthing the word *Later*.

It took an hour for Rabbit to calm down again, and I didn't begrudge him the time. We made our way back to his room upstairs where Mark had somehow gotten a few toys and stuffed animals in for him. Between spikes of extreme emotion, it was like he was catatonic, staring off into space and thinking Lord only knew what. I used one of those gaps to excuse myself to the bathroom—running downstairs to get the silver that I'd showed Mark last night, because my son still needed his 'vitamins.'

And Mark was there. Maybe he'd been lurking outside Rabbit's room this whole time—or the entire mansion was littered with cameras. "Hey," he said softly, like talking louder would make me run.

"Hey," I said back.

"Where are you going with that?" His eyes flickered to the small bottle I held.

"To give Rabbit some."

"I overheard, earlier. You'd really never told him before, had you?"

"No," I said and shook my head.

He walked past me and sat down. "I had to move heaven and earth this morning to get that contract signed, you know. I pulled every favor I had, and burned all sorts of bridges. If I didn't know the location of so many bodies, literally, I wouldn't have had a chance in hell. As of right now, most of the family thinks I've fallen for a stripper, and are expecting wedding invitations."

I gave him a weak smile in response. I didn't want to encourage him—and I was so tired of this breaking feeling in my heart.

"So—when are you going to tell him about that?" he said, pointing at the silver in my hand.

"I don't know. Not now, for sure."

"You can't hide it from him forever, Angie. He deserves to know."

Just because we were close didn't mean I wanted Mark's parenting advice. "How old were you, when you got big?"

He looked taken aback, and then considered. "High school, I think."

"Did knowing you could easily beat up people make you a nicer person?"

"No, but—"

"If I tell him about this," I cut him off, shaking the bottle, "it'll change the whole rest of his life. He'll never get to be a normal boy."

Mark didn't look convinced. "I spent my whole childhood wishing I could be Superman. Knowing that I was one would've made me a different man."

"Better? Or worse?" I pressed him.

"I don't know," he answered, honestly, I could tell it by his eyes. "But I would've liked to be the one making that choice."

I rocked back on my heels. "He's not ready for that, Mark."

"And tonight? When some magician shows up, along with the vampires who're taking a lot—and I mean *a lot*—of my money? What's he going to think then?"

"I don't know—we'll cross that bridge when we come to it."

"In eight hours," he pressed.

I finally broke. "Are you being a dick just to prove that you can?"

"No, I'm being a dick because I care. And because after tonight I won't get to see you again—despite the fact that there are Fleur hotels in many, many other countries." He stood and crossed the distance between us to catch my chin in his hand. "You're not alone, Angela—and it doesn't have to be like this."

I took his hand in both my own. "It does for right now, okay? Because if anything happened to you—"

"Unlike Rabbit, I'm a grown man. And you shouldn't get to decide for me." He stepped back, boring into me with his dark eyes.

I inhaled to fight him—and then realized he was right. He'd already done so much for me, risked so much—now that he knew, truly knew, what he was getting into, who was I to fight him?

Especially when I wanted to be with him so badly?

"Where are the other hotels?" I breathed out the words. Elation leapt into his eyes, then he tried to hide it, just as fast.

"Paris, London, Tokyo, Hong Kong."

I tried to imagine Rabbit and I in any of those places, and I couldn't—but I could imagine Mark there. And if he was there, maybe we could try.

He read my expression and rushed forward, engulfing me in his arms to spin us around.

"No guarantees," I said, leaning into him with closed eyes, feeling the whirl. This was what it felt like to be loved.

"I don't need them," he said, landing us both and brushing hair out of my eyes. "I just need to know that you want to be with me."

"I do." For better or worse, for even if it got both of us killed. "But you have to wait till I feel safe—I don't know how long it'll take."

"I don't care—as long as you're on the other side."

He kissed me then, the kind of deep plunging kiss that made you a little faint, and anything else I might've said was gone.

# CHAPTER SEVEN
## JACK

I drove up to Mark's suburb and parked far away from his house at eleven. I had a feeling someone would tow Betsy before I got back to her, but I bet the local guys here knew how to not fuck up older cars, and I wanted to get the lay of the land on my way in. This neighborhood of mansions were all carefully built so that the houses were invisible to one another. Mark's particular one was in a ruggedly dramatic spot, with desert on one side that didn't worry me —and dramatic hills on one side, that did. The wind was blowing the wrong direction for me to scent anything, but with Zach's blood on board, I was sure I could feel eyes.

I walked up the sandstone stairs to the palatial front doors and stood, waiting to be let in, knowing I was clearly visible on any number of security cameras. The door opened, revealing Paco inside. He gave me a companionable nod.

"This place is being watched," I told him.

"I know. I don't have to be like you to feel it." He set his jaw. "We've got three cars ready in the garage."

Because whichever car wound up heading to the bunker might get followed. "Good idea."

"I am a professional," he said.

"And...speaking of?" I tried to lead him.

"You're the first one," he told me.

"And you don't even have to be here," Angela said, holding a duffle bag, trotting down the immense stairs.

"I came to help."

"I don't want you putting yourself in danger for me, Jack." Her beautiful lips were pulled into a frown.

I ignored her. "Does the name Jonah ring any bells for you?"

"No—why?" Her frown turned deeper, and she raked her free hand through her blonde hair. "Just stop trying to help me, please, for your own sake."

"What, just because the last time I did got you assaulted by a vampire stripper?" I quipped, and then saw Rabbit coming down the stairs after her. "Oh, man, ha,ha—I mean," I started sputtering, trying to play it off.

"That's a bad joke, Jack," she said, giving me a glare. "Don't listen to him, baby," she said, as Rabbit reached her side. "And I'm serious —go home."

I shook my head. "I'm not leaving you with them alone. Besides, it's not like I'm missing any work."

"Incoming," Paco said, having gotten a cue from his ear.

The doorbell rang, and he went to open it, letting in a disheveled looking—well, I didn't know who. Or what. They looked like a cross between the cowardly lion and the scarecrow from the Wizard of Oz, come to life—a thing of fur and straw and brightly colored patches, walking with an odd herky-jerky mobility. I moved to put myself between it and Angela instinctively, and found Paco already there.

"What are you?" I demanded, knowing the thing was strange.

"He's my decoy," said an unfamiliar voice from behind all of us, as the door closed. We whirled and found a man there, beard and all, only he was dressed like a woman, with a corset and a skirt under long flowing robes. Behind him, Mark had his gun out, and cocked.

"How the fuck did you get into my house?"

The man sighed. "I'm Merlin, the Mixed Up Magician. You've seen my billboards on the Fifteen? Or the One-Fifty-Nine?" He looked at the zombie-walking stuffed animal and waved his hand—it fell to the floor with a solid thump. "I don't particularly want the Pack looking for me later, either."

"I have seen your billboards," Paco admitted, tilting his head. "And your show—I guarded a client there—you were funny."

The magician bowed to him. "Thank you! I didn't get best comedy-magician act of two-thousand-nineteen for nothing, even if the rest of you are apparently heathens."

"If you can transport yourself inside places, why did you even need that thing?" I touched the creature that'd lurched through the door with a booted toe.

"Because that," he said, while pointing, "smells like my greatest rival. And I will never, ever, pass up an opportunity to throw that man under a bus." He set his shoulders and looked around. "Now, shall we begin?"

"Mom?" Rabbit asked, a squeak.

"I'll explain later. I promise," Angela said and soothed his hair.

"I'm just here to do a magic show, little one," he said, and then began rummaging around in Mark's living room.

Mark kept his gun out and trained on the magician. The magician seemed unconcerned—I doubted mere bullets would do anything to him.

"Can I get two fingers of rye?" he asked, shaking an empty glass.

"Why, for a spell?" Mark asked.

"No, because I've been sober for twelve hours. It's really starting to drag."

Mark looked over, gave all of us accusing stares, and then put his gun away to bartend.

"So that's the magician?" Angela asked.

"Seems like it," I said.

"I've never met a magician before. I thought all magicians were men," Rabbit said, with the forthrightness of the young.

"Don't I look masculine to you?" the magician asked, sashaying up, his beard a stark contrast to his skirt.

Rabbit's brows pulled into a frown. "I'm not sure."

"Well, that's the point. There's a hell of a lot more magic at the edges of this world, then smack dab in its boring center. As a werewolf, I thought you would know, no?"

Angela's eyes about bugged out of her head. "He's teasing, Rabbit."

"Rabbit, eh?" The magician's kohl lined eyes gave him a knowing look. "I get it. Naming your child the thing you wanted them to be. My parents named me Charles. It didn't work."

"So—the ceremony?" I prompted. The bunker would be ready soon, and I'd feel a hell of a lot better once Angela and Rabbit were inside it.

"I've already begun. Can you feel the change?"

"The only thing I can sense is an increase in the overall levels of awkwardness in this room," Mark said, returning with a drink to press into the magician's hand. Merlin took it, slammed it, and then made the glass disappear.

"That's part of it," he explained. "If you're going to be a thing you haven't been before—it's going to hurt a little. Change always makes people anxious." Then Merlin licked all his fingertips and reached out to touch Rabbit's face in a complicated pattern.

"Mom?" Rabbit's voice rose.

"Shh," the magician answered instead.

"Mom, Buster doesn't like this!"

Angela didn't like it either—I readied myself to hold her back. "Just a little longer, baby," she promised.

There was a sensation in the room, of ratcheting tension. I felt it, Angela felt it—I could even see recognition in Paco and Mark. And then the magician stepped back, hands still frozen in the position they'd been holding on Rabbit. He walked across the room, arms out, like he was shooing someone away, then bent over and replaced his hands on the decoy's head. The decoy twitched and spasmed, shrinking in size and in height, until it was about a seven year old boy's dimensions.

"There," the magician said, when they were finished.

Angela leaned over, and breathed in Rabbit's hair. "He's...different. It worked!"

One of Merlin's eyebrows rose imperiously. "Of course. You're up next, Mama." He wiped his fingers off on the front of his dress, and then began licking them again.

I tried to read Angela's face as the magician lay his hands on her. She wasn't as still as Rabbit had been—it seemed like it was hurting her more, even though she didn't make a sound.

"Angie?" Mark asked, looming near in concern.

"I'm fighting the silver here," the magician grunted in explanation. "Years and years of silver abuse—she's like some sort of poison addict."

Angela's face flushed red then gray-blue, and the magician staggered back. This time you could see what he held—an almost perfect representation of Angela, like the finest sheer silver cloth in his hands. Merlin walked it over to the decoy and let it drop, where it covered the thing like a shroud before disappearing.

Angela sagged. I caught her without thinking, and after that, breathed her in. The change was subtle—but there. I took another long inhale, of her neck and her hair—and looked up to find Mark giving me a death glare.

"And with that, I'm done," the magician announced.

"It worked?" Paco asked.

"Yeah," Angela whispered. She leaned into me for a moment longer, then caught herself, moving to stand on her own.

"I was told to give these to you, once the ceremony was performed," Merlin said, handing a slip of paper to me. I flipped it over and found the coordinates to the bunker. Then Merlin walked over to the original decoy and nudged it with a high-heeled toe. The creature lurched up, like a Rabbit-sized animatronic doll, with the addition of a stubby tail. "This is also yours—it'll smell like the boy did until dawn, so do with it as you see fit." After that, he wandered off, not away, but deeper into Mark's house.

"Where are you going?" Mark demanded without following.

"It turns out I phase best through wine cellars! Especially ones with expensive bottles of wine!" Merlin shouted back.

Instead of a response and instead of shooting anything, Mark just ran his hands through his hair. I admired his restraint, as Paco took charge.

"Three cars," Paco said, taking the addresses from me. "One with Rabbit, one with Angela and that thing, and the third one as a lure."

Angela knelt down and started digging through her bags to give the decoy some of Rabbit's clothes. Rabbit knelt down beside the thing and poked it. The thing tried to poke him back. "You two are guarding Rabbit," she announced, looking over at Paco and I, as she tugged pants onto the monster.

Paco nodded, and I said, "That's why I came."

"And me?" Mark asked.

Angela shook her head, as she stood up again. "You're out. Because I love you. Please."

I watched him inhale to fight her and stepped in. "Everyone knows you mean well, Mark. And I know you're rich as fuck. But this —this isn't your game. I promise you, if you get any deeper into it, you'll die."

He pulled himself up to his full height in front of me, everything in his bearing full of threat. "I'm supposed to take life advice from the person who doesn't have one?"

In all of our other encounters, I'd always pulled back, trying to respect Angela's choices and Mark's space. But this time I held my own, occupying more space like I might just before fighting, and when I spoke I let a little of the *hunger* through. I knew it made me sound more ominous. "Just because I'm dead, doesn't mean I'm wrong."

He didn't back down, and his voice went cold. "You let anything happen to her and I don't care how undead you are, I will hunt you down and make you pay."

"You're a man of your word. I would expect nothing less."

He surveyed all of us with a disapproving shake of his head. "This way to the garage."

ANGELA FOLLOWED Rabbit to our car, pressing his head to her stomach. "You be safe, Rabbit. You do what these men tell you, okay? Especially Jack." She knelt down to be on his level. "And if anything bad happens—you run."

"Where are you going?" Rabbit wasn't scared—I got the sense that he liked adventure—but he was confused.

"To the same place you are, sweetheart."

"Then why aren't we in the same car?"

"It's complicated." She kissed him. "But I love you. And you're going to be safe, all right?"

He nodded back at her, for her sake, even though there was no way either of them could know. "I love you Momma."

"I love you too." Her eyes on him were wide, as though she were drinking him in. "I'll see you soon." Paco gently grabbed him, and guided him into the back of the car as she looked to me.

"Anything you want to say, I already know," I told her.

She nodded briefly, then rose up on her toes to kiss my cheek. She didn't shock me this time, but the action did, it was unexpected and it caught my sated hunger off guard, so I could appreciate it as a man might and it took my breath away.

"Here," I said, coming back down from the surprise. I leaned down and pulled the silver knife out of my boot. "Just in case."

"Thanks," she said, taking it carefully.

After that, after the door to our car was closed, she returned to Mark and kissed him—the kind of kiss that was so intense you felt like you had to look away from it, even though you wanted to watch.

He held her head gently afterward and whispered something until she nodded, and got into her own car.

Mark walked up before the garage doors opened and knocked on the back passenger-side. Paco rolled the window down and spoke first. "I suspect this terminates my service to you."

"Not as long as you keep them safe. Report back when you can."

"If I can," Paco corrected, because he wouldn't do anything to sabotage Angela's future freedom for my sake. All that was in me wanted to reach over and squeeze his hand.

"Fair enough," Mark said, and nodded. He nodded to the other car as well, and inside the darkly tinted windows, I thought that I could see Angela wave.

Paco tapped his radio. "Roll out," he said, and the doors lifted, letting all three cars out into the night.

# CHAPTER EIGHT
## ANGELA

The decoy-thing sitting beside me in the backseat stank. A little like Rabbit, but more like something *wrong*. It was hard not to recoil from it, but I had to pretend that it was my baby boy. I couldn't even look back as we left—one of Paco's men had counseled against it—as it might break the illusion that Rabbit was here beside me.

There was a chance that Mark's place hadn't been under surveillance, but all the men in the car found that thought unlikely. Anything they thought past that, they kept to themselves.

We traveled in tight formation until we hit the highway, and then the third and unimportant car zoomed ahead. It took an exit and I was sure I could hear distant motorcycle pipes.

"Go," one of the other men commanded—and our car surged off. I could almost feel Rabbit's car pulling further behind me—and neither my wolf nor I liked that one bit.

My wolf—suddenly she was back inside, filling me, now that the magician had lifted all that silver out—and she was pissed. This thing beside us was not her cub, and her place was at his side. My lips peeled back and I almost snarled.

*No, no, no*—I wrestled with her, internally—but based on what was happening now and, goddamn the timing, an almost full moon outside—she wanted to be in control. She'd been hidden inside me for long enough and it was going to be her turn. She was going to make the decisions here.

I was utterly unprepared for how strong she was with all my silver gone.

I reached for the knife Jack had given me, unsheathed it, and batted its blade against my hand. "Stop that," I warned, in an effort to gain her attention as the silver bit me. She growled inside, and made me throw the knife down. Frightening things were happening in me—I could feel her strength—but I could also feel her claws—I held onto the seat ahead of me tight, like I was going to be sick and—

We were side-swiped.

Airbags blew from all over, pinning each of us in safety. My arm flew out for the decoy—I was a mom, and it was child-sized, I couldn't help myself—and I felt it flop against me with its doughy shape. Metal scraped metal as whatever'd hit us didn't stop pushing —then we were hovering over an edge, I could feel us teeter—I had half a second to scream-howl before the stomach wrenching sensation of freefall.

The sedan landed, on its roof, with all of us, still seat-belted, dangling inside.

The way Paco's men recovered was extraordinary—it was just that the car was besieged by werewolves in an instant. A door was pulled off, and the man next to me shot out—until an arm reached in and clawed his throat out, spattering the interior with his blood. There were two heavy thumps as other creatures landed on the chassis of the sedan above—I went for my seatbelt to free myself as an almost disembodied hand reached in and yanked the front passenger outside. I heard him howl and then a crunch. I could see the silver knife glittering, just out of reach.

I had a feeling, from my wolf-driven senses, that most of the Pack was here—which meant that Rabbit had escaped. And he would be safe as long as no one knew where he'd gone. The driver'd freed himself and was bravely preparing to charge the outside world.

"Give me a gun?" I whispered. He handed me one. "I'm sorry," I said—and then I shot him. The Pack was going to kill him anyways —but this way he couldn't tell them where Rabbit was, first.

Hands reached in, caught my ankles, and dragged me out.

"What the fuck is this thing?"

Pack members had pulled the decoy out after me, and Murphy stood over it, kicking it with his boot. It tried to fight him but lacked strength, instead puffing out sooty blackness like a mushroom. Then —it blossomed. Like one of those disgusting black snake fireworks that stain your sidewalk on the fourth of July—the decoy erupted, winding up around Murphy's legs. He started to scream and it flowed into his mouth.

"Get it off me! Get it off!" he shrieked, before he started coughing up blood.

Men rushed in only to be burned themselves; shouting, rubbing their hands against their jeans or in the dirt at their feet. All the silver that'd been living in me was slowly killing Murph now. I bit back a howl of satisfaction. He fell to the ground and started rolling, trying and failing to put out the fire inside.

A non-descript black truck pulled up, and Daziel leapt out of the cab, running over to help Murphy before other Pack members held him back for his own safety. When Murphy was done screaming, clearly dead, he wheeled on me.

"What're you smiling at?"

"Murphy, getting what's his at long last," I snarled.

I could only see him out of my one good-eye, as the other was swelling shut from the tumble I'd taken in the sedan. My hands were being tied in front of me by someone I didn't know—there were ten or so pack members here, most I didn't recognize, it'd been too long.

Daziel looked me over. "You don't look very good, dearie."

I could see his mutilated hand, from where Jack had gotten him. "Yeah? Would you say I take after my mom?" I grinned so that if he slapped me he would cut his hand on my teeth.

His eyes narrowed. "Get in the truck."

"Or what?"

"Or we'll drag you behind it."

Men I didn't know grabbed me, boosted me up, and shoved me inside the truck's cab, pushing me until I reached the center seat. No one bothered putting a seatbelt on me, and Daziel jumped up and into the driver's seat.

"Nice hands," I said, as he reached for the wheel, noticing the missing fingers Jack's silver knife had taken off of him.

"Shut the fuck up," he said, and someone yanked a hood over my head.

THE TRUCK BOUNCED along whatever path Daziel drove it—I knew we were going up from the way I slid back, and from the way my ears popped when the altitude had changed. While I knew the Farm I'd remembered had been raided by the cops, I was sure they'd found an alternate location, someplace else safe they could hide on a full moon night.

And speaking of—my wolf knew one was near. She'd retreated when there'd been speaking to do, but now that I was in darkness, I could feel her responses to our situation battering my mind. Each twist of the truck unnerved her, the loud sound its clattering made, the way that strange smelling men pressed up on every side. I had no idea how fine her nose could be, until now—I could scent each man in the cab individually. Each man and...his wolf. Their wolves were always present, always close at hand. Whereas the transition between me and my wolf was like switching gears—they, and their creatures, lived as one. I found myself jealous of their simplicity and also scared by it. I was literally in a truck cab full of wild animals.

The only thing I was truly sure my wolf and I had in common was our concern for Rabbit. We were not as one, and I didn't think we'd ever be, but our love for him bound us inextricably. If they had him, I was sure Daziel would have gloated by now—*please be free, baby, please be free.*

The truck lurched to a stop, and we were yanked out. Someone caught us before we fell over—Daziel—and someone else pushed us along—he smelled gamey, so in my head I called him Meat.

"Stairs," Daziel warned before I reached them, and then we walked up and in through an open door. Meat's hands caught our shoulders and shoved us down into a chair, and then the hood was removed.

My eyes adjusted to the dark far faster than they had any right to. We were in a garage, and a massive cage occupied half the back wall.

"Where are we? And what are you going to do to me?"

Daziel counted on the fingers he had remaining. "We're deep in the woods, love. And now we're going to make you pay."

I squinted at him. "You didn't have to drag me here for that. You could've shot me beside the car."

"Too easy. Plus, we want answers. Where's the boy?"

"I don't know."

"I had a feeling you'd say that."

I waited for someone to dramatically run one of the wood saws in threat, but all of them seemed unconcerned.

"I honestly don't know where he is. And you'll never find him again. We changed our scents."

"I can tell," Daziel said, tapping his own nose. "But you'll be able to find him. As your wolf."

I was taken aback, and started shaking my head as he went on. "She grew up away from her kind. Poisoned with silver. Taught to hate us, to be afraid. You think our wolves can't sense the fear in you for yours? You've been practically torturing her the past seven years. What do you think will happen when she comes out? Will she believe you? Or will she listen to us—when all her instincts tell her to rush to his side?"

Blood started thundering through my veins. I hadn't gone through all this to not keep Rabbit safe—

Daziel stood. "I've a mind to take the price of Murphy's death and my hand out of your hide. But Gray still wants you whole—for now. Get in the back," he said, and I knew he meant into the cage. I hesitated.

"GET IN THE BACK!" he shouted, and both my wolf and I jumped. The remaining fingers of his bad hand snatched my hair up and threw us forward, onto our hands and knees—we had to lopsidedly scramble with bound hands for the cage's door. He came into the cage after us, which we realized with a panic—and then a boot came at our face. Between it hitting and our head ricocheting off the metal bars behind us, everything went black.

# CHAPTER NINE
## JACK

"Can I have a gun?" Rabbit whispered from his position between Paco and I on the floor of the sedan we were being driven in. I looked down at him.

"No."

"Jack," he pleaded.

"Remember at Happyland? I saw you on the Space Police game. You've got no aim."

Paco looked over at me, flashed me a brief smile, then returned to scanning the outside world. Ever since we'd lost track of cars one and two, it'd been smooth sailing, worrisomely so. Either there'd be a hell of a lot of werewolves waiting for us at the end of this—or they were all off chasing Angela. I rubbed at the planchette beneath my shirt like it was a worry-stone, feeling the tingle of it rocking back and forth as the silver burned me, as fast as I could heal.

We drove outside of Vegas proper, then north, and by then it was clear we weren't being followed, unless werewolves had figured out how to be invisible. Rabbit fidgeted and I patted the center seat. "Come on up." When Paco didn't fight me on it, I knew he was thinking the same.

Rabbit sat in between us and dutifully put his seatbelt on. Looking across him, to Paco, I realized that this singular moment might be the closest I ever got to a normal life. We looked like a little family, me, the man I loved, and some kid we'd gone and adopted. I snorted at my foolishness, and Paco looked over.

"What?"

I grinned at him. "Nothing."

One disbelieving eyebrow rose on his forehead, then he went back to scanning the horizon.

THE ROADS we were on were obscure. Between the desolation and the shanty-like shacks we passed, that could hardly be called homes, we looked like we were on our way to a horror movie set. Which was fitting, considering.

"Where are we?" Rabbit asked. He wasn't tired at all—I wondered if that had something to do with the moon in the sky.

"A hideout."

"Where's Mommy?" He twisted in the seat to look behind us.

"She's going to meet us there," I said. But given that we'd left at the same time and the fact that you could've seen brake lights for miles out here—

"Are you sure?" he asked, looking up at me.

"Yeah," I lied. It's just as well he wasn't mine—I would've made a shitty dad. Paco frowned, but otherwise was quiet.

FIFTEEN MINUTES AFTER THAT, the driver slowed and stopped outside an RV trailer in front of a large pile of worn boulders. The only sign of life was the generator running beside it, sputtering diesel fumes into the night.

"This is it?" Paco asked.

"Purportedly," said the driver, unwilling to commit.

It didn't look like a bunker, but then again, I assumed it wasn't supposed to. "Let me go in first," I said, seeing as I was 100% more danger-proof than anyone else in the car, Rabbit aside. I got out, closed the car door quietly, and heard Paco relock the doors.

The trailer was old and rusty. There was a cistern on the roof for water, and all the wheels had been replaced by cinderblocks and brick—its travelling days were done, which was good, because it looked like it would crumble if I knocked too hard. There was nothing outside of it that had even the smallest hint of welcome, not a potted cactus or a welcome mat, so if this wasn't Rosalie's or one of her employees, I was going to get shot.

I walked up the rickety stoop and lightly knocked. "Hello?"

The blinds covering the door's window didn't open, but the door did. "Jack," a familiar voice said. "Come on in."

Maya stood there, wearing the most clothing I'd ever seen her in —jeans, a tank-top, and her fire-engine red hair was pulled into a high ponytail. No make-up, either. If we'd been at a party and I didn't know who she was—and what she was—I would've definitely tried to get her number.

"This is it?" I asked, leaning in, and looking left and right. The inside of the trailer was as dated as the outside was, all done in '70s shades of brown and orange.

"Would I be here, otherwise?" she asked, rolling her eyes at my foolishness. "Get your people—have them hide the car out back. There's some tarps by the boulders."

"Cool," I said, and jumped down the stairs. There were thirty long steps back to the sedan, and I knew what I had to do. I opened the back door.

"Is Mommy here?" Rabbit asked.

"Not yet, kiddo," I said, reaching in to pull out his bag.

Paco put a hand on his seatbelt, as did both of the men in the front.

"*Stop. None of you move,*" I commanded all of them, and Paco looked up.

"Don't you dare," he growled through gritted teeth.

"I'm being nice by explaining it to you. I don't want you to think I'm an asshole later."

"Too late," he hissed.

"It's too dangerous here. I read Mark's contract." I grabbed Rabbit and picked him up. "He's covered—you're not."

"Are you?"

"I forgot to have him put that clause in there. Next time."

I could see Paco struggling to move—if he could free himself from his seatbelt, or reach his gun—I leaned into the car and spoke directly to the driver. "*On the count of three, you can move. But you will only turn around and drive this car back to the road. After that, all of you will forget where this place is—that you were ever here.*"

"*Goddammit* Jack!" Paco said.

"Love you, baby—one-two-three-go!" I said, pulling back from the car and slamming the door behind me. The driver put it in reverse and soon the only thing that hinted they'd been there was a lingering cloud of dust.

Rabbit watched the car go away. "Why'd you do that?" he asked.

"Because I wanted them to be safe."

He blinked, looking up at me. "Don't we want to be safe?"

"It's complicated." I took his hand, and we went up the trailer's steps together.

I INTRODUCED Rabbit to Maya and while he was polite, he didn't leave my side until I physically sat him on the couch, in front of a TV and a cable-spool repurposed into a coffee table, then I pulled Maya into the small kitchen.

"Cute kid," Maya said.

"Yeah." I'd looked and listened—we were the only things moving in here. "So where's the other guards?"

"Tamo's coming around four in the morning, once he's done with his shift."

I didn't like the thought of spending the end of the night—and a full day—with Tamo, but he *was* a strong motherfucker. "Then I'll head back," she finished.

"Wait—so there's only going to be two of us here? At any time? Didn't I mention a werewolf army?"

She laughed and stretched, cat-like, then popped the knuckles on both of her hands. "I'm good for at least ten. Aren't you?" I fought not to grind my teeth. "Besides, we have opposable thumbs. And the floor of this place is now insulated with weapons and silver bullets, courtesy of your woman's man's money," she said, tapping her heel on the ground with a hollow thump. "Rosalie still has a business to run. She can't leave it vulnerable, Jack."

"Fine, whatever." I would replace any number of guns with a few loyal vampires—but loyal vampires were hard to come by. "Where's the bunker?"

"Here," she said, walking into the living room, where Rabbit was fidgeting on the threadbare couch. She turned, to make sure she had both of our attentions, as though she were doing a magic trick—and then unscrewed the top of the coffee table, lifting it up to set aside. "Voila."

I'd thought the coffee table was hillbilly chic—but inside it hid a metal tunnel, like a storm drain. As for what was below—I snapped my fingers and listened to the echo. It wasn't deep, but it was dark, and it smelled of rust, dust, and old blood.

Maya leapt inside and I heard her land. "Come on, Jack," she said —and Rabbit was already peering over the edge. She flipped a light switch and there were a series of pops in succession, as old-fashioned light bulbs turned on, and she walked down a hall, out of sight.

I hesitated, unwilling to leave Rabbit behind and worried about putting him in danger—and then he decided for me—throwing himself over the edge, to land super-hero style at the bottom of the shaft.

*"Wait right there, or else,"* I growled at him, and quickly dropped in.

By the time I reached the stone floor, Rabbit had realized he literally couldn't move. I could see panic in his eyes and feel his blood surging. *"You can move now.* Just—be careful," I warned.

He shuddered suddenly, dog-like, a full-body thing. "How did you do that?" Rabbit looked from me to himself and back again. His eyes were full of fear and more than a little mistrust.

"I can explain later, all right?" *Please get here soon, Angela, before I have to explain vampire things to your boy.*

"You're just discovering what I always knew about your Uncle Jack," Maya said, coming closer. "He's no fun." She walked her fingers cross my chest and made Bella's silver planchette sizzle.

I inhaled and exhaled. "Let's get on with this, shall we?"

"Of course," Maya said, giving me a glittering smile before leading us down the nearest hall.

The 'bunker' was really an old mine shaft. Nevada was full of them, they killed a few adventurously foolish people every year. The trailer provided cover and an excuse for the generator that powered lights—along with a fan or two, I could feel their breeze.

"Most of the entrances were filled in for safety reasons," Maya said, pointing at a few rubble walls. "There's drops down here even we couldn't survive, and tunnels too deep to leap out of. And this is where you'll be sleeping during the day with Tamo." There was a star-burst of corpse-shaped impressions carved into the stone floor, with thinner slabs of stone nearby to be dragged over like heavily starched blankets. "You haven't died in darkness until you've died underground."

I couldn't help but notice Rabbit hanging back. I hoped I hadn't ruined whatever fragile bond we'd had. I could've told him to forget it, but I didn't want to go messing with his head—and he deserved the truth, besides. I just wished I'd been able to ease him into it more gracefully.

"And this is where we'll put you-know-who during the day," Maya said, tilting her head toward an alcove that had metal bars, lockable from the inside. I assumed they'd be giving Rabbit the key, that was something at least.

"Who's going to guard him?"

"True believers."

"Huh?"

"Like Tamo. They're in for the cause."

I fought not to roll my eyes. "What 'cause?' The fattening of Rosalie's wallet?"

"Oh come on, Jack," Maya said. "You know what they want. Eternal life, same as us."

"Same as you, maybe. You were there when I was turned, remember? I didn't get a warning."

"Oh, that's right. I forgot. You're so high and mighty, Jack. You didn't want this gift, you just had it *thrust* upon you—and now you're an ungrateful man-child who's upset that he can't always have his way." She didn't have to raise her voice—her hissing vituperations echoed in the small hallway. "You don't even realize how goddamned lucky you are."

"You call living this life lucky?"

"Your version of it is!" She took a step forward and got in my face. "You don't have to sleep where she sleeps every day, and wake up to hear what she's decided for you every night! She chooses where I go, what I do, who I dance for, when I feed!" She stabbed a finger at my chest and I let her. "Whereas you get to have your own place, drive your own car, and keep your own money—you live your own life! If I'd known I was signing on to be eternally babysat, I would've just stayed home!"

I took a step away from her and found my back against the cold stone wall. I'd always assumed Maya enjoyed her role in Rosalie's life. Shows how little I knew.

"Jack!" Rabbit's panicked voice echoed back from up ahead. "Jack!"

Both Maya and I looked at each other, and then started running for him.

"Rabbit!" I shouted after him.

"Shut-up! Cave-ins!" Maya hissed again.

He was two turns ahead of us, standing naked inside a room that also had metal bars embedded in the wall—but this time the lock was on the outside.

"Rabbit? How did you?" I boggled, knowing his ripped clothes were in a pile near my feet.

"Jack-Jack-Jack, get me out!" He reached through the bars with all of his body, but he was trapped by the circumference of his ribcage, just an inch too wide.

I grabbed hold of the lock and tried to wrench it open—but the thing was solid steel, as wide as my palm. I looked to Maya. "Go get the keys."

She wasn't listening. Her eyes were wide, staring at something behind Rabbit—something faintly moving.

"*Jack!*" Rabbit pleaded, still stretching his hand out for me. The chamber behind him was like something out of a haunted house. It held a stone coffin, with one tiny hole in the top, and an ever-so-slightly tilted slab. There were grooves carved all over it, and the whole thing was wrapped in chains.

The lid on the coffin was moving too slowly to see—but all three of us could hear it, as stone ground over stone.

"*Go get the keys,*" I growled at Maya.

She was so panicked she didn't yell at me for trying to whammy her. "I can't! I don't know where they are! Rosalie's the only one who feeds the Sleeper!"

The sound of grinding continued—was it just my imagination that it was speeding up?

"Jack!" Rabbit howled in panic.

70

I squatted down to be at Rabbit's height. "How'd you get in there, buddy?"

But I knew the answer as I asked it. The clothes at my feet were ripped—Buster must've gotten curious.

"I just—it smelled weird—and I wanted to know more—and," He looked down at his little naked body in dismay. "What happened to me?"

Angela had never told him he was a werewolf? *Christ.*

"I'll tell you everything, but first I need you to calm down." I was tempted to whammy him, but I didn't think I could command him into changing. I didn't know how hard it was to change or how often he could change—Angela should've left me with a rule book. "Take a deep breath," I said, looking him in the eyes and taking a deep breath myself. He mimicked me, as best he could. "Okay. What happened right before you found yourself inside there?"

"Buster. We were talking and—he—I knew he knew how to get in. So I let him." He leaned forward, pressing his head against the bars. "I was a wolf," he whispered, his eyes begging me to believe him.

"I know," I said back. "And if you're going to get out of that cage, you're going to have to become a wolf again, Rabbit. Just for a little bit."

"But—" he protested.

I held up my hand for silence. "It's your power, Rabbit. Just like I have mine, you have yours. You can do this. I believe in you." The grinding sound continued, an ominous undercurrent to our conversation. "Buster's been with you your whole life, hasn't he?" I asked, and Rabbit nodded. "He's not just your imaginary friend, Rabbit—he's your best friend, truly. And he would never let anything bad happen to you."

"I think he ranned away," Rabbit said, tears squeezing from his eyes, his words regressing in his fear.

"No. Never. I promise you." I moved to sit down and took Rabbit's hand, pulling him with me, on the other side of the bars. "Changing might be scary—I don't know what it's like myself—and so maybe it scared him, or you, you know? But it's natural. You both did it once. You can do it again. Close your eyes." Rabbit did as he was told, and I took both his hands. "Repeat after me. Buster, I need you to come back now."

Rabbit intoned the words, just after I said them. I looked over at Maya, who caught me looking and then made a gesture, holding her hands up to approximate how much of the coffin was left to open before whatever-the-fuck Rosalie kept inside it came out to visit us.

"Keep repeating my words, Rabbit: I'm sorry I got scared, Buster. I've never turned into a wolf before. But I really need to turn into one again, now."

Rabbit repeated me, emphasizing the *really*. His tone had begun to match mine, along with his breathing.

"Okay, keep your eyes closed. I'm going to count backwards from ten, and when I reach one, you're going to turn into Buster. I want to meet him, okay? Don't try to force him out—just relax. Keep breathing. Ten. Nine."

I started going in descending order, a long breath in between each number, matched by the rise and fall of Rabbit's little chest. What was I going to do if this didn't work? What kind of damage would I do to him if I just yanked him through? How could I ever face Angela if I could only give her half of the corpse of her dead son?

"...three. Two. One."

Both of us waited in silence. I only had eyes for him, staring at him as if I could will him into changing—and then he did.

It was like when a magician flips a sheet out from underneath a table full of glassware. One second, his skin-side was out, the next, it'd been ripped away and replaced with fur. It wasn't a silent process though—the sound was as sickening as the grinding of the stone behind us was—pops and snaps, like breaking twigs, and a soft squelching that spoke of the movement of flesh.

At the end of it I was looking at a wolf, roughly the same size as

Rabbit, behind the bars of the cage. I stood up and made room, and he trotted on through, the metal stroking him on either side.

"Nice to meet you, Buster," I said. He came up to me, intelligent eyes staring up, and sniffed at my hand. The grinding sound inside the cage stopped.

Maya put her back to the bars and sagged down them to the floor. "Rosalie is going to kill us."

THE THREE OF us jogged or trotted back the way we'd come. I hadn't considered the reverse problem—how to get Buster to turn back into Rabbit—but maybe staying a wolf was safer for now. At least it didn't require clothing—his first change had turned Rabbit's outfit into rags.

When we reached the exit, Maya and I looked to one another. "Want to just stay down here?" she asked.

I shook my head. "Not really, no."

If she jumped out first, she could trap us in—if I jumped out first, she'd be back here unsupervised with Rabbit. Why was it that every interaction with another vampire had the beginnings of a 'you have a chicken, a wolf, and a bag of grain' riddle in it?

"Ladies first," I said, deciding to take my chances.

Maya gathered herself, then leapt for the edge and pulled herself up.

"I don't suppose you can jump that far, eh?" I asked Buster. Not getting a response, I said, "Don't hate me for this," and scooped him up before he could fight it, flinging him up and out of the tunnel's entrance—leaping up and behind myself.

"Ow!" Rabbit complained, from where he'd landed, back to being a boy.

"Welcome back," I told him, as Maya quickly screwed the coffee table's lid back on.

Rabbit looked around at the trailer. "What happened? Where's my clothes?"

The duffle bag Angela had sent with us was still on the ground—I dug through it and tossed underwear, jeans, and a t-shirt at him. "Here."

He pulled them on, all boyish and shy around Maya who was sitting on top of the coffee-table, looking pensive. "That was close."

"What was that thing?"

"Rosalie's pet."

"Is it safe for us to go back down there?"

"You and I, yes. And him, during the day."

"I'm not going back down there," Rabbit announced, jumping his jeans up. "Ever." He stood and looked at both of us, hands on his hips, in imitation of who knew how many adults. "Where's my mom?" He looked between us for answers—and when we came up short, he crumpled and ran into the back.

"Rabbit," I called after him, standing. Maya caught my arm.

"Let him run ahead a little—kids need space."

"Getting too much space is what made me, me," I said, shaking off her arm and heading after him.

# CHAPTER TEN
## JACK

The trailer only had one other room, so it wasn't like Rabbit could hide from me. I caught up with him as he was centering himself on a dingy bed, his back pressed up against the wall, curled up with his knees under his chin.

"Where is she?"

"I don't know. She was supposed to meet us here."

"Why isn't she here then?"

*Because the bad guys got to her, presumably.* "I'm not sure, Rabbit."

"Well—we have to go find her! We need to help her!"

"I don't know where she is." I held up empty hands.

"Ask that stupid magician for help!"

"I don't happen to have his number," I explained, trying to keep him calm. "We're outside of phone service besides, and we have no car."

"If she's in trouble, then we have to do something!"

"Your mom's tough. She can handle herself." I sat down on the bed, far away from him. "Our job is to keep you safe."

"Like from that thing?" he asked, pointing a dramatic hand down to where we'd been.

"Yeah, actually. How the heck did you wind up inside that cage?"

He made a face, wrinkling his nose. "Buster wanted to smell it."

"Well, not all of Buster's ideas are good ones." I assumed werewolves aged at the same time as their human hosts, because I doubted Buster was a dog-year's forty-nine. "Lesson learned."

Rabbit sighed and slumped forward, picking at lint on the sheet in front of him with one hand, while he threaded the other's fingers through his toes. "How come now?"

I inhaled. I thought I knew what he was asking, and dearly wished Angela were here to answer him instead. "I don't know, really. But you've been a werewolf your whole life. So's your momma."

His eyes flashed up at me. "Really?"

"Yeah."

"But—then—why didn't she ever tell me?"

I winced. "I think she thought she was protecting you."

"From?"

"From chasing after stinky things? I don't really know, Rabbit."

"From the bad guys," Rabbit said with a knowing sigh. "My daddy's alive—and he's a bad man." He watched me carefully to see what effect his words would have.

"I know—and he is, Rabbit. I'm sorry. You deserve a good dad."

There was a long silence, during which I could almost hear him think. "Are you a magician?"

"No. I'm a vampire." No point in lying now.

"Huh," he said, not entirely surprised. "S'prolly why you smell a little dead, then."

"Yeah?"

"Yeah—that other lady too."

I made a show of sniffing under my armpits. "I don't know...." I caught him thinking about smiling, before he rolled his eyes.

"It's not bad. Just a little sweet. I don't know why I could never smell it till now." It didn't seem wise to tell him it was probably because his mother had fed him silver. "Do you have fangs?"

"Like a snake's."

"Can I see them?"

I leaned forward slowly, mouth open, like I was going to show him, and then pulled back, snapping my teeth together. "No. They're not toys. Sorry."

"Aww!" he complained.

"It's time for you to get to sleep." I started tugging the sheets out from underneath him.

"I can't sleep—there's monsters!"

"We're monsters too," I said, gently unfolding him into a prone shape.

"But what about Mom?"

I paused. What about her? We hadn't really discussed what to do if I was on my own. I wasn't cut out for this. "I'm worried about her too, Rabbit. But let's give her the rest of the night."

"If she's not here by morning, can we go after her?"

"I'll be asleep then, sorry. But if she's not here by tomorrow night —we'll figure out something, monster to monster, you and me."

A whole day was much too long, I could see it on his face—and what was worse, I agreed. But we were too far away from civilization to do anything tonight.

"I'm not tired," he said, as I stood.

"Pretend to sleep until it works then. I'll be right outside the door."

"Swear?"

"Swear." I smiled at him as warmly as I could, and then closed the door behind me.

"MISSED YOUR CALLING, EH?" Maya asked when I returned to the living room. She was sitting on the couch, with a beer in one hand, and her heels on the coffee table.

I took a seat on the couch's far edge. "I doubt it."

"Me too," she said. "Tamo's on his way by now."

"Great," I said, my voice flat.

"What's the beef with you two, anyways?" she asked, while scooting closer on the couch, like it was Netflix night and we were more than friends.

"If he never told you, I'm sure as hell not." I stood, found no room in the place to pace, and so circled around, to sit down on the couch's opposite end, as she laughed.

"You don't have to be so prickly all the time, Jack. Not everything has to be so black and white." She stroked the wide end of her beer from her knee down to her hip. "I mean, come on. Look at me. Any red-blooded man in the world would be interested in this. And I think you've got a little red-blood inside you still, don't you?" She leaned forward and set her beer down on the table. "Come on, Jack, aren't you the least bit hungry?"

I leaned toward her slowly, with intent—and then reached over her to take her beer. "Nope," I answered with a swig. "I don't really like you and I definitely don't trust you, Maya. So, no—what I feel around you is the opposite of hunger. Unless a perpetual urge to break your neck is sort of the same thing."

She leaned forward fearlessly, her expression betraying no emotion. "You're just jealous I got to fuck your boss before you did."

My hand tightened on the beer bottle as I made a strangled sound. Somehow, among everything else that'd happened, I'd completely forgotten. "Yeah. About that," I began—then the sound of an arriving truck cut me off. The engine stopped, boots stomped up, and the door swung open, revealing Tamo, in shorts and a Hawaiian shirt. Guess he was off the clock. And over one of his shoulders, he was carrying something—someone—wrapped in plastic tarp. The wind outside changed, and wafted in the scent of fresh blood, just as I noticed some dripping from the tarp.

"Did I interrupt something?" Tamo asked, looking between us like he was the inopportune-timing-man on a shitty sitcom.

"Absolutely not," I said, rocking back. I kept hold of the beer bottle, it was the closest thing I had to a weapon.

"Take the top off, baby," Tamo said—and Maya leaned forward to do just that, unscrewing the coffee table's top again.

"Who's it for?" she asked, flipping the lid to one side, giving Tamo her best wide-eyed innocent girl look.

"For whoever wants some. Can't go into this thing hungry. Plus, he's juicy," Tamo said, hopping into the well. Maya hopped right in after him.

I could feel my fangs begging to bud—if I hadn't drank from Zach earlier tonight, they would've. As it was, the scent—there were openings in the mine below, there had to be, fans or vents—the scent of fresh blood washed back over me in an intoxicating wave.

The scent of blood was so fresh it was clear its owner was alive. I knew he—or she—wouldn't be when they left here. Normally I'd do something about that, but Rabbit's safety depended on my silence. So instead, I leaned over the tunnel's edge, trying to ignore the primal way my hunger stirred and the isolating feeling of being left out.

Maya returned before Tamo did, looking up at me with a blood-induced swagger, and I would've sworn that her color was slightly more pink. "Make way," she said. I did, and she sprang out—no need to catch the side and pull herself up now. "That," she said, rolling her head around her neck, "was tasty."

Her eyes flickered over to me, where I must've been looking at her like a dog watches from under the table. "Oh, go. Just because you're awful doesn't mean I'm going to slaughter a child."

"*Swear it,*" I said, using my whammy on her.

"I'm here for the money, not for the blood," she said.

"*And you'll protect him from Tamo?*"

"Goddammit, Jack—yes."

I knew she was compelled to tell the truth. Before I could second-guess myself I jumped in.

The warren of tunnels below now had irregularly shaped spatters of blood every few feet. I followed these like clues until I found Tamo, lounging against a wall, wiping blood out of the corners of his lips with thumb and forefinger. "Jack," he said warmly.

"Tamo."

"I left you some." He tilted his head into the darkness behind him.

"Barely." The life I sensed behind him was on the wane.

"Well, you are last. Besides—I thought that wasn't how you rolled?"

"It's not."

"So you're just down here compromising your morals for...."

"Curiosity."

Tamo laughed. "Good thing you're not a cat, Jack."

"Where'd you get him? Or, her?" I had a sudden irrational fear that it was Angela in the next room—but Maya would've said something, and I definitely would've smelled her—

"From just outside. Snooping around. Probably one of Sangre Rojo's crew."

*Red blood?* "You mean there's more than one vampire gang in town?"

"There's a lot more going on here than you realize—then you'll ever realize, given the glacial rate at which you choose to realize things." He kicked himself off of the wall. "Have fun with the dregs—I'll be heading upstairs."

I didn't like him being up there with Rabbit without me, but I did believe Maya, so I took a tentative step toward darkness and death.

"I can hear you," whispered a dying man in the dark.

So they'd left him his throat. "Hey," I said, like I was meeting him at a coffee shop. "Sorry about all this."

"Fuck you," he said, and snorted softly.

Here he was, all ready to die, and I was interrupting him. All the same, I felt the need to absolve myself.

"Look, I can't save you. I'm sorry. There's extenuating circumstances going on above. I'm watching a friend of mine's kid. I can't put him in danger for you, and that's all there is to it," I said as I walked in. "Is there someone you want me to let know that you died, once you've gone?"

He took so long to respond, I would've feared him dead already if I couldn't hear his heartbeat. "Are you one of them?" he asked.

"Yeah."

"And they left a child in your care?" He sounded incredulous.

"I get that a lot."

I heard chains shifting—I had no doubt he was tied down to a table similar to the one in the room with the Sleeper. "There's a lighter in my pocket. I want to see you."

I walked up to the table fearlessly—there was nothing he could do to hurt me here. I patted him down, found his stomach wet— blood, or worse?—and then found the outline of a lighter in his jeans. I tugged it out and flicked it on.

He had been an attractive man before all this began. In size, he was somewhere between Mark and I, well-muscled, with an assort- ment of tattoos—including two huge swords streaking down each forearm. He had shoulder-length hair, brown or black, hard to tell, it was damp with blood—and there was a huge gash across the front of his chest, down to his stomach, like he'd fought a car-sized cat. I had a feeling his guts would pop out if he coughed wrong.

"Are you telling me the truth?" he asked. One of his eyes was swollen shut, the other inspected me for signs of lying.

"I am." I brushed some of his wet hair off of his face.

"And you would never hurt Sam?" He strained his head forward.

"Whoever they are, I promise." The flame went out, and I flicked it on again. "I'd cross my heart, but I don't think you'd believe me. Where can I find them?"

"You won't have to. Sam'll find you. Trust me." He sagged his head back against the stone. "What's the kid's name?"

"Rabbit."

He laughed again, sick and wet. "Yeah. You wouldn't make up a name like that."

"No, sir, I would not. What's yours?" My free hand found his and held it. It wouldn't be long now.

"Bryan. And I just put a string of explosives around the perimeter of the boulders. We've been watching this nest for weeks."

I blinked and leaned forward.

"Saw it get busy last night and today. Weapons coming in, believers wandering about. Thought we'd take it out tonight. Burn everyone inside and blow the tunnels. But none of our intel said anything about a human child." His eyes stared straight up, he was using all his strength to speak. "It is human—right?"

"Yeah." Rabbit was close enough. "Why're you telling me all this?"

"Not allowed to kill bystanders. Sacred pact." His voice fell to a whisper. And I realized that seen from a certain angle, as the lighter's flame played over his skin, the swords on his arms looked a hell of a lot like crosses.

"Even if it means that vampires escape?"

"Sam'll handle it. No one escapes Sam." A mysterious smile played across his lips and then he was dead. His heart spasmed, searching for blood to pump, and finding none, eventually stilled.

The lighter was burning me, I didn't notice it—until I smelled the stench of burning flesh. I let it go out and licked my thumb, knowing it would quickly heal.

I put the lighter in my pocket, and left the man behind.

As I LEAPT into the trailer's living room, I heard a car drive off. "Rabbit?" I said without thinking.

"Still asleep," Tamo said, from the couch. He'd turned the TV on —this shithole somehow had satellite. "Maya went back."

I picked up the coffee table's top and set it down, like I was recorking a bottle of wine, and then moved to stand as far away from him as possible.

"What, you don't like me?" He popped his feet onto the table and straightened out his Hawaiian shirt. "What's not to love?"

"Don't pretend we're friends, Tamo."

"Why wouldn't we be?" The look he gave me then—it went on half-a-second too long. "I mean, we both work for Rosalie," he went on, and gave a self-deprecating laugh. "Some of us harder than others."

"The only person I actually work for is his mother," I said, jerking a thumb back to the room where Rabbit slept. "Your—girlfriend? That's more like slavery."

"You keep saying things like that. Rosalie's right. You're never going to appreciate the gift that you've been given."

I crossed my arms and leaned back against the kitchen counter behind me. "Probably not."

"That still doesn't mean that we can't be friends, though, Jack. Forever's a very long time. Forever gets lonely." He sank deeper into the couch and gave me a pitying look. "I mean, it is what it is now— you're one of us, even if you don't want to be. And it's not all bad. I mean, if you were still human what kind of help would you be to your wolf-woman?"

I refused to respond, even if he was right.

"And this might be the first time you've ever been financially helpful to Rosalie. So it's a win-win, really."

"It didn't help her when I took out the Nevada Thirteen?"

"That was a one-time deal. Whereas this new club—it promises to be *lu-cra-tive*." He said each individual syllable like it was its own word. "This is a tougher town than it seems, Jack. Rosalie's already reinvented Vermillion a few times, but it's hard—either steam runs out, or you push too hard and risk exposure. Add in the hassles of upcoming technology, and Rosalie needs to make money to invest now, while the getting's good."

"So what—in twenty years, she'll disappear and then return, pretending to be her own daughter?"

"Something like that," he said and shrugged. "Or she'll go elsewhere and start again. And take me, of course."

I squinted at him. "And the rest of us?"

"I don't think you'll live that long," Tamo said, and then laughed and laughed.

# CHAPTER ELEVEN
## ANGELA

In addition to the eye I could no longer see through, I woke in the cage with an incredible headache. I came to with my cheek against solid concrete, facing one of the massive lag bolts that fastened it to the floor.

"She lives," said someone behind me. I rolled over, slowly, and found Meat on the other side of the cage, sitting in the chair. Another pack member was pacing nervously, behind him.

"What time is it?" My jaw felt rickety.

"Late."

I scooted myself upright, and rested against the cage's bars. "I don't suppose I could get some water?"

"Sure," Meat said, heading out to return with a bottle and washcloth. He tossed them through the slats of the cage. "For your eye."

"Thanks," I said, taking a gulp, and then pouring some out onto the washcloth and putting it on my face.

"You shouldn't be talking to her," the other man—not much more than a boy himself—said.

"Shut it," Meat said, and the other man did. I wondered what Meat's wolf was like—he was an unassuming man, wiry and tan, with a leonine amount black hair, and a chin-strap beard ending in a goatee. He didn't look that different from any of their other members, but I had a feeling that seniority here was not based on age, appearance, or time-served—it was all about your wolf.

"Not much of the old crew left, eh?" I asked, after dabbing cold water at my eye.

"Werewolves and gang members aren't known for their longevity."

I smiled at him and snorted softly. "Now that's a three dollar word, coming from a one dollar mouth."

"I'll show you what you can do with your one dollar mouth," the other man started for the door of the cage, one hand on his belt. He was so thin he looked like he could slide through the bars if he had to.

"That's enough, Holt."

"You're not supposed to be talking to her!"

"Says who?" Meat asked, brows high.

"Daziel."

"Get the fuck out of here," Meat said, so low it was almost a growl. From the look on Holt's face, I knew Meat's wolf was several ranks higher than his own.

"Fine," he said, spitting through the slats of the cage at me, before storming off.

"Sorry," Meat apologized, once Holt was gone. "Murphy was his friend."

"Once upon a time, I thought that too." I pressed the wet fabric to my eye again, and tried to stop from hissing.

He watched me and shook his head with a sigh. "You know your wolf'll heal that, if you let her."

"Yeah?" I asked, peering at him with my one good eye.

"How do you think we survive the transformation, if not by healing?"

I shrugged. "I've never transformed before."

His eyes weighed me, then decided I was telling the truth. "That's sad."

"Not really. I had a life."

"You mean being kidnapped and hanging out with strangers in a garage isn't your idea of a good time?" he asked with a tease.

"Definitely not. Different priorities."

The water did make my eye feel better. And Meat, whoever he was—I couldn't see his name on his vest, because of his hair—didn't currently seem threatening. I knew that could change though—I'd seen the look in Holt's eyes. "So what now?" I asked.

"Now, we wait."

"For?"

"For them to spring him."

I swallowed, my mouth suddenly dry. "Who?"

"You know who," he said.

I did. Gray. Out of the prison infirmary, and then back into my life. Acid rose in my stomach as my heart started to race.

"So you're really his woman, eh?"

"No, I'm not." Without meaning too, my voice laced into a wolf's growl, as if I was answering for the both of us. Meat looked a little taken aback, but regrouped quickly.

"You know you can't hide from him forever. You belong to him, until he dies."

"Has anyone ever explained to you how utterly misogynistic your werewolf bullshit is?"

He slowly nodded. "Yeah. Because if they can't find Rabbit...the plan is to keep you in here." He looked around to indicate the cage and the surrounding garage. "And let Gray mate with you until you give him another son."

The human part of me wanted to throw up in disgust, but my wolf—I lunged forward, faster than I'd ever moved in my life, and with more strength than I'd ever felt. I wound up against the bars of the cage, reaching out for him with a clawed hand, and I could've sworn I felt the entire cage move with the force of my landing—and where it hit me, didn't hurt. Meat didn't so much as twitch, despite the fact that my hand was just inches away from his knee—he just watched me with glittering eyes.

"I promise you I will die first, even if I have to claw my own neck open," I growled.

He took a measured inhale. "I believe you."

I pulled my hand back through the bars and cradled it to me like it was a child.

"Feeling better?" he asked, and I blinked at him—with both eyes. The swollen one was healing. I cupped it, and swore I could feel the lump recede.

"Yes."

"Told you."

"I didn't transform."

"Not all the way, no—but she's there, inside you. I can feel her." He tapped his own chest with one hand, the home of his own wolf. "She wants to get out."

Now that I was silver-free—I could feel her too. Restless, yearning, like the delicious way Mark would make me feel right before he put himself inside me, hopeful, hopeless, happy and scared. "Yeah."

"Full moon's in two nights. Your transformation will go a lot easier if you've already tried things out. Trust me."

So would any attempt I made on Gray's life. As a human I was helpless, but if I had teeth and claws—"How?"

"Take off your clothes," he said, and I frowned at him. "Do you want them to get ripped up?" he asked. "No. So take 'em off. And then, let go."

"You just want to see me naked."

"I'm not complaining if I do," he said, his face still stoic.

What's the worst that could happen? I'd be sitting here, straining nakedly, for five minutes, and then he'd laugh? My hands went for my shirt, and I turned around.

He moved as it came off, I heard his leather crinkle. "Gorgeous work," he said, when my tattooed back was exposed.

"Thanks," I said, unlatching my bra. In seconds, I was naked—and I didn't want to turn around. "Now what?"

"Like I said—let go."

*Let go.* Like it was that easy. I'd spent my life collected, eyes on the ground, one step after another. I hadn't relaxed in so long, having to take care of Rabbit, my mother, my business—I couldn't even remember what it was like. Except for those brief moments with Mark and sometimes, in my dreams. When *she* was there.

I closed my eyes and let the wolf-dreams come. The feel of the wind brushing through fur I didn't know I had, the scent of the garage—old oil and sweat—the piercing sensation as bones and teeth moved—

"Oh God," I hissed.

"She's not trying to hurt you," Meat said from somewhere nearby. "Stay calm."

I'd had enough tattoos to know how to swallow down pain and pride. My eyes rolled closed and I went to that place deep down inside me where it was always quiet and always dark and where nothing mattered anymore and—

*We* looked out. Of *her* eyes. They were lower—we were roughly at the level of Meat's now fragrant to us crotch. My body wasn't mine anymore, it was hers, and it was strangely glorious—my world would never be the same.

"Good girl," Meat said, moving to a squat. Through her eyes I could see the wolf inside him—shaggy and black, with a chest like a barrel. And while I wanted to be angry at him for keeping us locked in here, she nudged her muzzle through the bars and licked out at him. He reached forward, carefully, and set his hand on us, we felt it thump against our side, a million different nerves messaging as he stroked fingers through our fur, and scratched fingernails down our back.

And then something snapped. I woke up again for a second time, on a concrete floor, only this time I was naked. "What the fuck?

What just happened to me?" I bolted upright, scrabbling for my clothes.

"Easy," he said, waving a hand. "You just changed was all. And now you're back, you're you."

"But what happened?" I scrambled, pulling my shirt on without a bra.

"You only switched over for a few minutes." He tilted his head to look at me. "Have you ever gotten drunk enough to feel like you're time traveling?"

I shook my head and he snorted.

"Well, you're missing out. But it's like where you have that one shot too many at the bar, and then ten minutes later you're getting a blow job in your truck cab—even though you don't remember how you got there, you know you must've said something right to the lady, and managed to walk out with your keys."

"If you say so," I said, yanking my underwear up.

"It's disconcerting, at first, but when you get used to it it's just part of the flow."

I'd gotten back to fully clothed. "So—I really did it? I was her?"

He was crouching now, beside the cage. "Yeah. And pretty sexy, if I do say so myself. Actually, not me, my wolf—we, uh, get along. I had a feeling we would. Wade told me about you."

"Did he now?" I asked archly. "Which part?"

"The part where he taught you how to do tattoos." He gave me an easy smile. "I always wanted to do art myself, but I'm no good."

"Not the part where he raped me?"

Meat looked aghast. "Did he know you were Gray's woman?"

"Gray was in prison." I stood and hopped back into my pants.

"Wade was like a father to me," Meat went on.

"Hello—werewolf lifestyle equals pretty fucking rapey. You know what happens to the girls you get pregnant, right? The ones who don't make it?"

He had the decency to look embarrassed. "Yeah. I always make sure to wear condoms."

"Hooray for you," I said.

He stood and back away and I knew I'd lost whatever progress with him I'd been gaining. He sat down in his chair, flipping back his mane to reveal his name patch. *Jonah*. What the fuck—how had Jack known that name? And just what had Jack known?

"I didn't ask to be bitten in, you know," he went on. I was going to point out the huge discrepancy between his situation and mine, but held it back, because sarcasm wasn't going to gain me any sympathy. "Some guys get formal invitations—I got initiated at a brawl. Wrong fight, wrong time, and then I'm here."

"You seem to be doing well for yourself."

"If I was, I'd be out with the rest of the old guard, springing Gray."

I sat back against the bars with a thump. "What's it like, taking orders from someone you've never met?" He frowned, but had the wisdom not to answer. I couldn't help but push him. "Or rather, what's it like, taking orders from someone you've never met—knowing that he killed Wade?"

Meat—*Jonah*—went still then, but his nostrils flared, and I knew from a hundred different signals that I had his full attention, and that he was trying to read me.

"You didn't know, did you? You must not be in that loop," I said.

His eyes narrowed and he looked down his nose at me. "How would you know what happened?"

"Because Wade Davis's severed cock wound up on my doormat as a peace offering." I rocked my head back into the bars behind me. "Gray's not the flower-sending type."

I wanted to gloat with all my might—to cheer myself for the blow that I'd landed, even behind steel bars. But instead, watching him, I felt bad. The pain of my packmember...hurt me. We were connected, he and I, no matter how much I didn't want to be.

"I'm sorry," I muttered—but I meant it.

He stood and left the garage without a word.

· · ·

I CLOSED my eyes and cursed inability to keep my damn mouth shut. When Jonah returned in five minutes, with two other men plus Holt again, I went into the exact middle of the cage, where no one could reach me, and I made myself small.

"Tell them what you told me," Jonah commanded.

I looked up from the ball I'd tucked myself into. "Why?"

"Because they need to hear it from you, not me."

"Why?"

One of the men made a dismissive sound, as Holt said, "I told you she's a bit—"

"Gray sent me Wade Davis's severed cock," I interrupted him. "In a box. With a love note. Asking me to come back to him."

Holt's mouth snapped shut, and Jonah nodded. "Thanks."

The four other men looked to one another. The expressions on their faces were jumbled but similar—upset that I'd confirmed some long held fear, or relieved that they didn't fear without reason.

"That's heavy," said the stocky and bald man standing closest to the door.

The odd thing was, they all seemed to be taking my words at face value. I stood and took a careful step forward. "You're not worried, not even a little, that I'm lying to you?"

"That'd be a pretty crazy thing to make up, and you don't seem crazy," Jonah said. "Plus—it's hard to lie, wolf-to-wolf."

"Then how come no one told you?"

The men looked at one another. "It was Mags who brought him in," Holt said.

"And he wouldn't think to question whatever Daz told him to tell us," Jonah said.

"I take it Mags isn't a wolf?" I asked.

"Not yet, he ain't," answered Holt, apparently forgetting that I was not to be talked to.

"Not ever, now," threatened the fourth man, who'd previously been silent. He was very tall and unnervingly attractive in a stern way, with heavy brows and a chiseled profile.

I looked between their number and realized two things simultaneously—that they would believe whatever I said next, and that what I was going to say next was true.

"If you let me go, I promise I'll come back, come full moon."

I had all four of their attention, mixed with scoffing and astonishment.

"You hate him and you don't even know him—I do, and I hate him all the way. Let me fight him." I wanted it all—I wanted Rabbit, safety, Mark, and there was only one way that I could get it.

"He'll kill you," Jonah said.

"Better that than this, here." I shook myself against the bars. "And you know it," I said, and hoped they really fucking knew that that was true.

"But he's our leader," Holt said.

Jonah looked to the other three men. "For now."

"If I kill him for you, then you don't have to," I said, letting my wolf's whine crawl into my voice.

"She's not even pack, Jo—I can't believe you're considering this," the bald man said.

"She is *too* pack," he protested. "I saw her change."

"More pack than Gray is, off in his own goddamned cage," said the tall one.

The other two remained unconvinced—but the fact that I'd convinced two so readily gave me hope. "I am Pack. And I can show you," I said, ripping my clothing off.

"You're not going to be able to do it again so quickly," Jonah warned—but I was already shutting myself down, running for my silent space. *Please, wolfie.* Rabbit had had a nickname for his wolf since he was three—where was mine? *Wolfie—show them—come on.*

I felt her rise inside me again, trying to flip me inside out, trying to show them the fur hidden in my form—but it wasn't working.

*Please.* I have to get out of here. And I have to come back and end this—however it will go.

I cried out for her in my mind, and she tried to rise again and—

93

she held steady. Just underneath my skin, inhabiting my body without twisting it into her form. Her eyes were the ones that looked out now—for me they were only windows. My wolf tried to open my mouth to explain, like she knew I could, but she couldn't—my wolf had no words.

But they did.

"She did it," said the handsome one. I twisted toward him and saw the glimmers of his wolf inside. My wolf had been alone for so long—but she didn't have to be alone anymore. She leaned against the metal of the cage, and the smooth cool brushed my sad furless skin, making my nipples hard.

"What if this is some kind of game, or prank?" said the bald one, still by the door.

"Wolves don't know how to lie," Jonah said. His hands were on the edges of his vest, waiting, weighing.

She pushed a hand out, and I could feel her thinking that hands were the only good thing about this form, the way they could reach and grab. She reached out for him—and then she shoved at the lock of the cage. She was Pack. She wanted to be outside. To meet so many wolves and then be forced to be so separate—it was cruel.

And they knew it. The bald one set the lock of the garage door he guarded behind him, just as Jonah came up with the keys for my cage. My wolf could scent the wolf in him, and she leaned forward to breathe deep, eyes closed, feeling the cage's metal vibrate as the lock shifted open behind her. The cage door slid back, and my wolf was free.

# CHAPTER TWELVE
## ANGELA

My wolf luxuriated in my body, feeling my human form for the first time. She ran her hands over herself, ecstatic to finally get to *feel*. I felt such an upwelling of power trapped inside her, as she possessed me. I felt her fearless strength permeate every pore.

Then she looked out at the four of them, these first wolves she'd *really* gotten to meet, face to face, and despite being new as a pup, and trapped in my human, I knew she'd never been more sure of herself. She stepped out of the cage and surveyed them.

My wolf reached out for the tall one's cheek, drawing fingertips across it, feeling the stubble of his beard, before hooking a finger into his mouth to draw him near. And as he stepped, he *shifted*. I no longer had to wonder what his wolf looked like—I could sense it, underneath his own skin, same as mine.

"Jo," Holt warned.

"I know. I feel it too," Jonah said, as I brought the tall one closer. His wolf smelled like sage and was tall, just like him. She released his mouth and nuzzled up to his side, feeling the smoothness of his leather against our skin, the strange way the metal bits on it puckered up against us. She brought up a handful of his hair to breathe, and again felt the stubble of his chin as he stroked his cheek up mine.

"If we do this," said the guard by the door. "There's no going back. We'll be traitors."

"Will we? She's pack. If she says she'll return at full moon—I believe her," Jonah said.

"But she's Gray's woman," Holt began.

The three of them were quiet, as my wolf pushed her hands up through Sage's hair. She bit lightly at the end of his chin, because she could.

"Gray killed Wade," Jonah said.

"Fuck Gray," said the bald guard. And for them it was decided. I could feel them shift with delight, and turned. Jonah's shaggy beast came up beneath his skin, and his eyes went feral, just as Guard's stocky body was inhabited by a surprisingly lanky tawny wolf.

More of my kind. My wolf practically wanted to cry with delight. They crowded me, and I loved it, breathing in all of them. Their hands reached for me as mine did them, begging each of them for more skin, and soon all of them were naked and we fell into a pile on the ground, rubbing and nuzzling one another. All my wolf wanted was to breathe them in forever, to carry their scents with me always, to know that she finally belonged.

And then, Jonah's wolf nipped at my ear. She swatted him away, while the others snuggled on—but he did it again, this time running his tongue up from my neck to my throat. I twisted toward him, my wolf biting her teeth in the air at him, in mockery. He grinned, then tried again—and this time, put his teeth on my throat, and kept them there. My wolf went still as primal and instinctive things rose inside us. Sage pushed at Jonah. Jonah growled in warning, and Sage pulled back.

My hands went for Jonah's hair, feeling it flow over me, falling against my neck and breasts. My wolf rubbed it against herself, making us smell like him, and he released me, looking down at me, jaw slightly dropped, and there was a new scent in the air—arousal. His—and mine.

He moved down my body, as the others released me, knowing what would come next. He crouched over me, licking from my neck down to my breasts, out to my armpits, and back again, as though he were cleaning us before we could be touched. My wolf kept one hand in his hair and used the other to stroke the light fur covering his body, and as he made his way lower our legs parted open for him naturally.

He ran his face through the short hair that covered the space between my legs, burying himself in my scent, until he stepped over and knelt between my thighs, mimicking the shape of his wolf on all fours. Our legs spread even wider in hope and then—as though he were going to drink from a pond—he lowered himself and began to lap.

Human lovers had done this to us a hundred times, and yet the second his tongue touched me, I knew this would never be the same. He was tasting me, testing me, I could feel his tongue roll and probe, his lips pull and suck, all the while as he breathed me deep. He wanted all of me, and he was starving—he even licked lower and back, picking my hips up to part my ass and lick my asshole, making me whine. As a human I knew I would've felt invaded—but his attention made my wolf feel complete. She didn't have to be alone anymore—*her pack wanted her.*

The pack I'd always been afraid of. The pack she'd never known.

She whined, communicating her sorrow through me, letting them know how long it had been, and how scary every moment was along the way. She'd wanted to do right by me, and by my child, but this whole time I'd been drinking poison to hurt her—it was my turn to curl up inside of her now, and be ashamed.

Sensations flooded her from where Jonah kept up lapping, and she made another whining sound. Someone whined back. I knew the same as she did just what they were communicating.

*Not alone.* She would never be alone again, if she didn't want to be.

My wolf looked up, and saw Sage crouched nearby, his long cock full, watching us with hungry eyes. Jonah saw my attention shift, and growled—and she fearlessly growled back at him.

They were equals. He was not in charge of her.

But he was in charge of Sage. Sage pulled back—until she reached out a hand. He came forward, head bowed in subservience, to sniff at it—and she used it to catch into his hair and pull him closer. He hesitated—and Jonah pulled up, to nip at our thigh. My wolf gnashed her teeth at him, in a playful silent laugh, but then he rose up and we saw he was not playing. His cock was wide and hard and straining. He had our full attention again, as he wrapped his arms beneath my legs to drag me up to him for mounting. My hips would've risen for him anyways—my wolf wanted him inside.

He put his hands on either side of my body, breathing hard over me, growling low, warning me not to move, and my wolf knew what he meant. She may not have been his for all time—but she was his for now. She growled back in answer, and he thrust.

His cock slid deep into my pussy, all the time he'd spent on it paid off—I was so wet and so ready and the way his cock seemed to lock in—I whined and rocked my hips against him without thinking. Men had entered us before, and my wolf had been forced to silently watch, but this—this was different in all regards. He smelled like wolf, and we smelled like wolf, and the familiarity—the sense of coming home—was dizzying. Jonah bit our shoulder as he thrust again, then went completely still.

*No!* I was so close to knowing what it felt like to be part of the Pack. He couldn't stop now. My wolf rolled our hips beneath him, begging him to fuck us hard. I whined, she whined, we both twisted and licked his lips, his cheek, his ear, rubbing our hands against his body, pushing myself into him. She needed him. She needed to be needed.

He held onto me, filling me without motion, as my wolf fought below him to get him to respond—and then she realized we knew other ways to be filled. They weren't wolf-ways, but—she flipped us, surprising him with our strength, so that we were now on top. My wolf arched back and rode him, grinding ourself against him, feeling the friction of his still hard cock—until he reached for me and yanked me down, holding me against him, my face to his chest. My wolf squirmed—*we were close! we were ready!*—and I shook my hair out of my face and spotted Sage again. My wolf looked at him and whined.

Sage came up, and this time Jonah didn't growl. He breathed against me, licking my armpit and my waist, and then went where I couldn't see him—until I felt his tongue against my ass. I whined, arching, full of Jonah but still ready for more. He nuzzled me there, licking hard, and then I felt his body move up over mine —over the both of ours—and his cock started pressing, asking to be let in.

Jonah held me tight, but I knew it was up to us to relax for this, if we wanted it—did we? My thoughts rattled around inside my wolf, like she was my new cage, and then settled, as she soothed me. Together, we were strong. Together, we could face anything.

She whined with my throat, and we relaxed, and he knew we were granting him entrance. He clambered higher and pushed, and we panted with sweet relief as his cock pushed in, creating a delicious stretching tension, and something about the pressure and the promise of release—it was like it was pushing my wolf and I into being one.

I moaned. I'd never held two cocks in me before, not even as a human—and I whined again, begging Sage to thrust.

But he went still, too, holding his body over mine, his chest at my back, his face in my hair, licking at my neck. Then he made a questioning sound, asking Jonah for permission, and while Jonah gnashed his teeth, he didn't growl—so Sage thrust. He moved the both of us, Jonah and I, and the sensation of him sliding in and out of my ass as I was stretched tight by Jonah was too amazing to be believed. I whined and held onto Jonah tight as Sage took another thrust, then a third, and then started rocking us.

*Yes.* This was what being a wolf was supposed to be like. I arched my ass higher, even as Sage's thrusts kept my knees splayed out over Jonah's hips, and let loose a small howl. Sage made the same sound in my ear—and we were joined by a third. Not Holt—but Guard. He came over, crouching low, his whole body asking for permission to watch me get fucked. Sage snapped his teeth at him, but my wolf agreed—she wanted him to see—she wanted everyone to know she had a *pack*. Guard came even closer, listening to me pant, and Sage grunt, and Jonah's silence, pushing his face in to breathe my same air. I licked Guard's lips and he licked mine—as one of his hands started stroking his cock in Sage's time. Guard saw me noticing, and gave me a submissive thrust, begging for a turn.

I rose up off of Jonah's chest, momentarily disturbing Sage's rhythm, and twisted, ever so slightly, to be angled—and I opened my mouth.

This wasn't something that wolves did. Mouths were full of teeth. But my wolf had seen me do it often enough and—Guard lay down, subserviently, and then scooted himself up, until his cock was in range, steadying it with one hand for me to take into my mouth, the ultimate show of trust. My wolf wrapped my lips around it and did so.

Guard whined in pleasure, as Sage howled again, continuing to pound, and every movement reverberated through me, Sage's cock pushing in, pulling out, rubbing me incrementally up and down Jonah's cock, my body rubbing against Jonah's as Sage's covered mine, and now my hungry mouth bobbing up and down on Guard's cock, licking it as Jonah had just licked me. Sage kept up his quiet howls, Guard kept grunt-growling, and even quiet Jonah—my wolf felt-heard him moan.

I was surrounded by *pack*. They were pleasing me, I was pleasing them—I lifted off of Guard's cock to lick Jonah's chest, to twist back and lick Sage's cheek, before retaking Guard again. Everything about this moment was good—my wolf never wanted it to end, and neither did I—and yet—somewhere inside me, heat stirred.

My wolf had felt this feeling come on from me a thousand times, but I had never once felt it come from her. She growled as she took possession of it, tensing. Sage sped up, and Guard brought his hand back in to stroke his shaft while we sucked on his cock's fat head. She growled again, feeling muscles tense, and fingers claw. Sage rose up, his thrusts buffeting, and we felt his teeth against my shoulder, preparing to bite—

But Guard came first, howling loud—cum jetted out of him, splashing in my mouth. We licked it off our lips as Sage growled at him, and then grabbed our hips and pulled twice before plunging himself deep, and savagely spasming against us. My wolf howled at her power over him as he bucked over me, lost in our ass, until he slid out of us and collapsed.

And now, we were just as it'd began, with only Jonah and me. Without Sage's weight behind me my wolf rose up again and pawed at his chest, and then lowered our head to lick his lips again. The hot feeling in us still remained, and still needed release. What good was a pack for, if not for that? We knew he was interested—his cock was still hard inside us—she nipped at his ear and whined and—

His hands went to my hips and held me there, thrusting gently up. After the barrage of sensations we'd had earlier, it was surprisingly delicate—and it let us feel the head of his cock, rubbing deep inside. My wolf whined, and Guard returned, nuzzling at our breast. My wolf rose without moving our hips and he moved to lick our nearest nipple, sucking. And Sage returned—crawling back to eat out my ass, as if kissing it for the gift it had given him. My wolf gasped, throwing our head back, biting at the air. It felt like bolts of energy were sizzling through my body, like we were standing on a mountain before a thunderstorm.

We helplessly rocked on Jonah's cock, feeling Sage's tongue play our ass, as Guard bit our nipple. Then my wolf felt our pussy clench around Jonah's cock, trying to claim it, and as she reached back to hold Sage's head right *there*—the sensations of being fucked, being sucked, being eaten—my wolf twitched and spasmed in my unfamiliar to-her-body, but it didn't matter, we were going together, there was no stopping now.

Waves of pleasure ran through us, from my nose down to where I knew our tail should be, again and again, like the moon-caused tide—and my wolf howled. Fully, for the first time. I knew she was proclaiming her triumph over these three, but also over me, the human, who'd kept her hidden for so long deep inside, and below me Jonah growled in deep satisfaction, at hearing me finally claim my wolf's side.

After that, we sagged forward and—it was me again. Alone. With a hard cock inside me and the sensation that I had just had an epic orgasm.

I was naked and straddling Jonah, my ass was sore, my mouth tasted like cum, two other pack members were naked, and the one that wasn't—Holt—was furiously jacking off. There was cum on the cement near him, he had to be on round two or three. He gasped sharply, then swayed like a willow tree, as another load left him.

"Oh God," I said. My speaking seemed to be the cue that they'd been waiting for—I could feel their wolves shift away, as much as mine had. I slowly rose up, and heard Jonah groan from below as his cock slid out.

*Had all that truly happened?*

It'd felt real, but distant—because it was happening to *her*, and not me—but I knew it'd been right.

"You went wolf," Holt said, shoving his dick back in his pants. "And then you all had an orgy."

I caught my breath. I believed him, even if my memories of the events were fading. "Why?"

"Beats me. But you all certainly enjoyed it."

"As did you," Jonah said, standing up. He grabbed a shirt off the ground to cover himself.

"That's mine," Sage said, and snatched it back from him.

*Sage?* I didn't know his name.

"Your wolf was lonely," Jonah explained. "She wanted to, uh, meet other wolves. And play."

I swallowed. "Play, eh?" I probably should've been horrified. But I couldn't shake the feeling that whatever had happened between the four of us had been right. And—the cage was open. I was outside of it, and none of them looked like they were going to put me back inside. "That's right," I said, remembering the last moments before my wolf had taken over clearly. "I was proving I was a wolf to all of you. Do you believe me now?" I turned, so that one by one, I could catch their gaze.

"Yeah," said the stern tall one. His patch said his name was Wyatt, and he gave me a lewd grin. "I wouldn't smell this much like you, otherwise."

I flushed, but I didn't look away. "And you?" I asked the bald guard.

"Definitely. My balls feel a quart low—and I know my wolf has good taste in women."

I looked at Holt, who was the only one of them still looking at me like he knew that I was naked. "If you're not a wolf, you're a witch. Either way, I believe. Also, I think you owe me a blow-job, for being a look-out while you all got your freak on."

"For being a coward," the Guard corrected. "I think I remember that part."

Jonah was the last of them and he was pulling on his jeans. If I'd done what it'd felt like I'd done with them—why had my wolf left him hard? I took a step closer to him—even though he was young, I had a feeling he was their linchpin. "And you?"

He nodded, pushing himself inside his jeans and zipping them up.

"Are you...sure?" I needed to hear him say it out loud so it would count.

"I was sure before—and I'm doubly sure now."

"Then—why?" I asked, glancing at the dent his hard-on made inside his jeans.

"I don't entirely know. Before I shifted, I told my wolf he had to protect you. He knows the score," he said. I could feel there was more to the story, and I waited quietly for it. "I always fuck girls with condoms on, I'm not an asshole. But this one girl—Bella—she meant a lot to me." His expression clouded with memories. "She begged me, and I wouldn't, but then one day when we were fucking she took it off of me, and I knotted her. It was an accident, but once I started I couldn't stop myself—and then she died." He swallowed and continued looking at the ground. "Her baby killed her, because of me. So I think my wolf just didn't want to hurt you, was all." He shrugged strongly and looked away.

And all the feelings I had about Willa came rushing back. How in love we'd been, up until our betrayal. I usually tried not to think about her, because thinking about her hurt—but it'd been another reason to hide from my wolf all along, since it had been a wolf that killed her.

"Thank you," I whispered.

"You're welcome."

"When I came here, with my best friend—lured here, by Nikki, more like—no one tried to protect us. No one warned us at all."

From this close to him, and with me still naked, I would've sworn I could feel residual electricity. I touched his belt buckle, half-expecting it to shock me.

"What're you doing?" he asked.

"Paying back your wolf."

"You don't have to," he said, with a headshake, but he didn't step away.

"It's not for me. It's for her." I undid his belt buckle quickly and pushed my hand inside the denim. His cock was still semi-hard and he smelled like me and—he pulled back.

"Why're you crying?" he asked.

I hadn't even realized I was. But the tears were there, just thinking of Willa, wondering how our lives would've been, if only someone had warned us. "Because I've lost a lot of people," I said, then took hold of the edge of his jeans again.

He brought a hand up, and wiped a tear aside. "Really—you don't have—"

"I want to," I interrupted, as I reached in. "Please." My fingers circled him before he could protest any further, and his eyes closed as he started to sway. He was erect in moments, back to the way he'd been before, when he'd been between my thighs, and he let out a low moan. His hand reached for my wrist to keep me steady while he thrust and—

"Oh God," he said, much as I had when I'd woken up. "Yeah—yeah," he hissed, and then his breath caught, and he grunted, releasing himself, his cum spilling out in my hand. He groaned afterward and slouched, still holding my wrist—for a horrible second I thought maybe he was going to throw me back into the cage. *And that had been a human thought*, I realized; my wolf knew better. Jonah just helped me wipe my hand on his jeans. "God—thank you. I don't think my balls have ever been so blue." He let go of my wrist and I took my hand back. "Plus, I'll be able to remember it," he said lightly, and snorted.

"As will we," said Wyatt, from across the garage, where he and the others were standing with their backs turned to us to give us privacy. "Are you two done? Because if the others get back—wolf or no wolf, if Gray sees her, he'll never let her go."

I turned around, still naked, among near strangers, and felt completely, oddly, safe. "Yes," I said, and started hauling on my clothes.

As we ran down the hillside, Jonah gave me driving directions: south and downhill, as fast as you can. After that, *follow my nose*. We crouched outside another garage, near a ramshackle farmhouse—

one with lights on, and people still inside. Three trucks were parked outside.

"Which one?" I whispered.

"Red one, closest," Jonah whispered back.

Wyatt caught my arm before I could run for it. "I'll go in and make a distraction."

"You smell like her," said Holt.

"We all smell like her," said Jonah.

"Bigger distraction then," said Wyatt, with a grin. He ran into the garage we were hiding behind. I heard an engine kick over—and then a dirtbike race out. He parked himself in front of the farmhouse, spinning in a tight circle, revving his engine loudly, howling, "Night ride!"

Jonah grunted, and looked to the other men. "Go get on bikes —now!"

They funneled away into the garage, as men inside the farm-house poured out, with shouts. Between the exhaust fumes and general confusion, it was perfect, and soon Wyatt had led the majority of the stationed pack away. I listened to the sound of dirt bikes receding in the distance, and Jonah stood.

"Anyone still inside is too drunk to care—you're safe."

It was hard to believe. "And you're letting me go."

"Till full moon, when you swore you'd be back here."

I nodded. But that'd give the others a whole two days to be upset at my absence. "What'll happen to you, in the meantime?"

"I'll tell the others that you swore." He shrugged one shoulder. Underneath the waxing moonlight I could see his face tense in concentration. More weighed on him than just my problems.

"And about Wade?"

"The ones that're ready to hear it, yeah."

There was something about him, so transparent and earnest, I felt like I had to tell him the whole truth. "It's my fault that Gray's in prison. My best friend and I—we were with him, and his baby killed her. When I went to the Farm to tell him, I found another girl's body, and reported it to the police."

"You were still human then. That was a human thing to do." He dark eyes flickered over to me. "And besides, he brought that on himself."

I had a sudden, unbidden urge to lick his lips in solidarity. *Where the hell did that come from?* "Thank you."

He nodded. "Go."

I RAN out to the line of trucks and found, as expected, the keys inside the red one. The engine turned over easily and I backed up, headlights off, using my own moon-enhanced vision to find the road. The path was twisting, I couldn't go that fast, and I prayed that Wyatt had taken the others off in the other direction.

Just as the road smoothed out and I prepared to hit the gas, a black wolf appeared behind me. It leapt and landed in the bed of the truck with a thump. I wheeled the truck sideways, heard claws scrape against metal, and the sound of growling from close behind. I drove wildly, trying to dislodge it, but in the rearview mirror I could see it shifting to take a human form—a naked woman with long black hair— who punched her way through the back windshield glass to grab me.

"I went out to smoke—I knew I knew your scent," said an inhuman voice behind me. I hit the gas again, as I struggled—but within seconds she'd pulled herself inside the cab with me, and was fighting me—bashing my head into the steering wheel and pulling the emergency brake, hauling the truck to a swift stop.

I recovered, far faster that I thought I could. "I remember you too, Nikki!" I grabbed her and shoved her back, hearing her thump against the passenger side door. She rebounded off of it to lunge back at me, and we wrestled. I elbowed her ribcage and heard things crack. She punched my jaw in retaliation, and we clambered in the small space. I kneed her between her legs, trying to throw her off of me, but only managed to throw her into the console. Her hands reached for and found my neck—as I shifted my hand into a clawed monstrosity without thinking, and plunged it into her side.

Somehow I knew—my wolf knew—that this was to the death. Blood gushed out of the wound I'd created, dripping down her arm, and I would've sworn that I felt organs inside her—human Angela would've thrown-up, if only she could breathe—everything was going black, and I could feel Nikki's own claws piercing my throat's cartilage on either side.

Then the truck rocked as something new scuffled on the bed—and both of us heard a panicked, "Mommy!"

Her hands on my throat paused—my hand inside her waited—and we exchanged a look born of maternal instinct. I had a finger looped around what I was sure was intestine, which the second before I died I would yank an armful of outside of her—and she was breaking my neck just as fast as it could heal.

If we did these things—we would both die, and neither one of us would ever see our children again.

"Mommy?" her girl—it was a girl's voice—howled, and I could see two small arms reaching in through broken glass.

Nikki's hands on my throat relented only enough to see if I would do the same. I pulled my fingers out of her side an inch in answer.

After that, we untangled in slow motion. Her hand reached for her side as she pulled back, and mine went for my throat, fighting not to cough now that I could breathe.

"Mommy are you okay?"

"I'm fine, baby," Nikki said, her eyes still on me.

I hated her. If she hadn't talked to Willa about Gray that day, then none of this ever would've happened—but I also wouldn't have Rabbit.

"Mommy who's that? What's wrong? Why're you fighting?"

"She's an old friend," Nikki answered.

"Yeah," I agreed, for the girl's sake. I spared a glance at her. She was as naked as we were—surely she'd chased after Nikki as a wolf —and she looked exactly like her mother, her black hair fading into the night behind her. "Get out of my truck, Nikki."

Nikki's jaw clenched in defiance—but if we fought again, it was even odds, and right now her daughter was foolishly reachable through the missing glass. Some part of me knew it was not unheard of for wolves to kill other wolves' puppies. That thought also made me want to vomit. I swallowed and sat up straight.

"I'm coming back on the full moon," I said, crossing my chest. "Wolf's honor or some such."

Her eyes narrowed, and then she slowly nodded. "All right." Her hand went behind her to find the door handle. I heard it unlock as she eased back out. "Get down from there, Lexie. We need to let the nice lady leave."

Lexie sprang from the truck bed to easily land at her mother's side. Nikki put a hand on her shoulder, steering her off the road, and I unbraked the truck to race into the night.

# CHAPTER THIRTEEN
## JACK

Tamo stopped laughing to give me a dangerous grin—and I heard the distant sound of a motorcycle engine, gunning in the night, nearing. "You fucker," I growled. He'd betrayed us to the Pack.

"Their money spends just as nice too, Jack. And what do you care, really? They want the boy alive. Too bad no one cares what happens to you."

I fell into a crouch, unsure. My hearing was good, the walls were thin, and the night was clear—the motorcycles might be miles off, yet, especially if they couldn't go off road.

"But the contract," I protested.

"Guarantees Mark's safety—since he's human. It has nothing to do with the outcome of all this—if it had, Rosalie never would've signed. How can she control what a pack of roving werewolves decide to do with GPS coordinates?" Tamo stood up, his bulk filling the living room. "Father-son reunions can be so emotional. Much like, I imagine, reunions between murderers and murderees."

My stomach sank lower and my balls rose. "You remembered."

"Of course I did. But unlike you, becoming a vampire has taught me patience. I knew if I waited long enough, my moment would come."

All the weapons and ammo were trapped under the floorboards of the trailer—which would be fine, if it weren't for Tamo. I needed to take him out one-on-one before this fight became one-on-four.

I lunged for him, fast as I could, faster than most humans could've seen—and he swatted me down with one meaty hand. He had the luxury of time and leverage.

"Really, Jack?" he said, sounding disappointed, as he drew his leg back to kick my head in.

I rolled away, breathing the dust of the trailer in deep. I punched through the floorboards, caught my hand on something and—found myself being yanked high, scruffed by the back of my neck.

"Do you miss your tricks? Where's your syringe now?" Tamo asked, shaking me mid-air, before flinging me aside. I hit the far wall of the trailer, rocking the entire shabby thing, before bouncing down. "This is the fight we should've had, Jack," he said, catching up to me—this time his kick connected, bending my body around its force, making my ribs crack. "I bet even as a human, I would've beat you." He lifted his foot up to bring it stomping down. I recovered enough to scoot away at the absolute last moment—and then grabbed for his knee-cap. I twisted it and pulled, like it was the lid to the coffee table. It slid underneath his skin and I felt ligaments snap.

He bellowed as his leg gave out, an inhuman sound—and Rabbit appeared in the hallway behind him. "Rabbit—run!" I shouted—as Tamo's fist clocked me. Teeth loosened and I felt my brain shimmy inside my skull. *"Ruuuun!"* I commanded, with a slur. I heard the front door snap open and then swing on its hinges, as Rabbit rushed out.

Tamo laughed again. "You're only buying him trouble—wolves love to hunt." He picked up my head like it was a basketball, one hand on either side, and lifted me halfway up, keeping me an arm's length away. "I've been waiting to kill you for a long time, Jack," he said as he began to squeeze. The pressure was amazing—I scrabbled at his hands as he laughed, taking his sweet fucking time, and I felt Bella's planchette swing, hitting different parts of my chest as I writhed in panic, burning me each time and then—I knew.

I ripped it out from underneath my shirt and raked it's pointed end as deeply as I could against the inside of Tamo's left arm, hitting bone. Blood spurted out like it was under as much pressure as I was, and he let me fall. I lay where I landed, numb, feeling the seams of my skull shifting back.

"What the—what the fuck did you do to me?" Tamo held the edges of the wound together, but they wouldn't seal, the silver burn was too deep. Blood was pouring out of him—his death would almost look like a suicide.

I gathered myself up to kneel. "This time I'm not making any mistakes."

"No!" He shouted—and fell on me. His greater weight took us both down, and we were wrestling on the floor in a growing pool of his blood. "I'm supposed to live forever!"

The only warning I had that he was about to bite me—to replace his blood with mine—was a sucking gasp as his mouth opened and he inhaled. I caught his hair with one hand and held his head up as he pressed down on me, fangs straining. Chunks of his hair tore out, along with ragged bits of scalp.

"No, you're not," I said—and shoved the planchette in his eye. He howled, as I pressed it in with my thumb, soft juices flowing out. His good hand raked down the side of my body, trying to cross over to reach my hand, but I felt the back of his orbital socket give—and suddenly I was holding up three-hundred pounds of dead weight.

I barely tilted him off of me. "Stay down, this time," I panted—while beside me his entire body went gray, like ash. Wind came in through the door Rabbit'd left unlatched and an inch and a half of Tamo blew away.

That was one way to make sure he was dead. I staggered to

standing, and kicked his remains, sending up a cloudy puff—just as the motorcycles landed. I could hear their kick stands lower and engines cut.

I waited until I heard feet up the stair to yank the lid of the coffee table off, and shouted, "Run, Rabbit!" down the tunnel like he was already inside—and the second they entered I leapt in.

I landed with a thump—half on purpose, so they would follow me, half because I was exhausted. My body had been healing on overtime—I didn't know what would've happened to me if I hadn't sipped on Zach. I staggered down the hall, using the sound of my own footsteps to listen for walls.

I was halfway down the main tunnel when I heard the first wolf land. I knew he'd shifted—there was a low growling sound clearly coming from an animal's throat, and I could hear his claws click on the stone. He scented me, he had too, and I was glad I'd let Rabbit come down the tunnel earlier. Even if Rabbit didn't still smell like his true self, maybe he still smelled like tempting little boy.

Where were the others though? Out in the desert? No—I heard another wolf land. And as the first two hadn't triggered any traps—they were joined by a third. I tried to listen for anyone else possibly moving overhead, footsteps thudding over the munitions under the trailer, and heard nothing. All of them were in here with me. Which was good, except—I didn't have much of a plan. I took off my boots and started jogging down the hall quietly in bare feet.

I knew I passed the cage where the Sleeper was, and wished to hell I could figure out a way to sic he/she/it on them—and the room where Bryan'd been too. The wolves followed behind me, equidistant, playing it safe.

Even though they were creatures of the night like I was, absolute darkness was something else. You couldn't help but think about the weight of all those rocks overhead, and how it seemed like the tunnel was narrowing. Soon I was in uncharted territory—the only thing that kept me moving forward was following a wisp of fresh night air. There was some way out of here, I knew it—I just needed to find it before they did. I raced down the stone halls, going deeper and knowing deeper was wrong—until the mine started bending back up. *Oh thank God*—if I was going to die, I wanted to die outside—the urge to escape being underground was primal.

I heard claws digging into the ground behind me and then a moment of silence—too long—and then a wolf landed on my back. It bowled me down, and I recoiled, just missing snapping teeth. It let out a finding sound, and I knew the other wolves were racing up, now that I was turned I could see-feel the space occupied by their blood-life. All three of them growled low, the sounds echoing in the small stone cave—and cave it was. It ended, here, I didn't hear any doorways. If I'd run any further, I would've hit a wall.

But that air! Where was it from? I could even smell plastic now—the scent of civilization, so close and still so far.

One of them leapt—I dodged and swatted him out of the air. I heard him hit the stone behind, and land with a pained noise, then rebound to join the slowly closing group. They had to know what I did—I could take any of them on, one on one, but if they fought as a group, I was fucked.

The only thing I had on me was Bryan's lighter. I pulled it out, closed my eyes, and lit it—I heard them snarl as light hit their dark-changed eyes, and I lunged. I swept the leftmost wolf into my arms, like I was giving him a hug—and snapped his back. I heard the sickening sound of it crunching and his subsequent howl. The nearest wolf jumped for me, and fastened his teeth into my arm before I could get away—I yanked it back, feeling the meat of my muscle rip.

"You going to become a vampire-wolf now?" I taunted, as the third one tried to circle me. I thought I could get away with the lighter-trick one more time, so I snicked it and—

Right behind his shaggy golden head I could see what I'd been smelling. There was a small tunnel, an old airshaft, and someone had shimmied down it to pack C-4 around the edges of its mouth.

If Bryan had managed to do that, then the hole was big enough for me. I'd left the lighter on, thinking fast. The two whole wolves were advancing and growling. Could they smell it? Did they know what it was, if they could? Were there thinking men behind their wild eyes, or was the change to wolf complete?

"Nice doggies," I said, patting the air between us. The one who's back I'd broken scrabbled his hindlegs underneath himself as his non-stop healing power reattached the severed endings of his spine. "That shit is just not fair," I said, sidling. I needed to switch places with them, so that I could reach the tunnel—but the way their lips seemed to curve into almost-human wicked smiles made my odds of accomplishing that minimal. The lighter went out and I put it in my mouth, talking around it like it was a cigar.

"The first fucker who bites me, burns. The next one, I pull completely apart. And the third, well—we'll see." I crouched low like I was going to attack them—and then raced for the airshaft's opening. I leapt up into it and caught my body on its sides and shimmied. My torso was in—as teeth mauled my leg. I kicked as hard as I could—teeth ripped, but their owner released me, stunned as I cracked his body like a whip. I grabbed up as far as I could and hauled myself—another wolf caught my ankle and yanked, teeth grinding against bone as I felt the crushing power of his jaws. I kicked him with my other foot, and felt my heel bounce over the socket of his eye. "Get off!" I shouted, grinding my teeth against the lighter's plastic case. He tried to snap his head back and forth, like a dog playing with a doll, and I could hear more jumping behind him—if I fell back now, I would be ripped to shreds. As he thrashed, he sent shockwaves through my body, whipping me from side to side in the small space and—I felt a cord at my back, so slim I wouldn't have found it if I hadn't been looking.

But I knew C4 always needs something to detonate it.

I shouted for strength and then pulled myself up further, holding not only the weight of my body up but also his. The action forced his furry head to cork the lower entrance, and I sent all my strength to my right hand. I let go of my left, reaching for the lighter in my mouth, and flicked it on. His golden eyes squeezed shut, as the whiteness of his teeth matched the whiteness of my visible bone.

"I fucking warned you," I said, and moved the lighter behind me. It caught my shirt on fire—but I heard the detonation cord take with a fuzzing hiss, like a bottle-rocket. I saw a streak of light and then the earth shook, with me inside it, as everything went black.

# CHAPTER FOURTEEN

## JACK

I woke up, surrounded by dirt.

All the nightmares that I'd ever had as a human—about dying, being buried alive—I was living them now.

My arms were bound—one overhead, one below—and neither of them could move. I attempted to struggle like some man-sized worm and got nowhere, only dirt into places it hadn't been before. I tried to shout but my lungs had been crushed.

I would've been dead a thousand times over if I were mortal, but because I wasn't, I was trapped here, in limbo, my own personal version of hell. I would die when the sun rose, and wake when it sank and I would *still be here*. For days, weeks, months. No one would care —and no one would find me.

How did vampires die? Could I starve to death? Would I dwindle? I could feel myself trying to heal the unhealable even now and willed my body to stop. Because why? What would be the point of living, if it was only this?

"Help!"

I managed to bellow it, more like a groan really, and dirt poured into my mouth. I would never shout again. *Oh God, oh God, oh God—*

# JACK

Time passed.

And I may very well have gone insane.

Because I could swear I felt something licking at my outstretched hand.

The insanity continued. Maybe this was what happened to vampires when they truly died, all the madness that their 'lives' created caught up with them, making them feel things that were impossible.

And then I felt something nip me.

*Oh God.* I was going to be eaten alive by desert rats.

I wriggled my fingers and found them free and tried to swat away whatever I felt, streaks of fur, wet tongue, sharp teeth.

What would protect me during the day? Nothing. I'd wake up tomorrow night—if there was enough of me left to wake up at all—with my hand eaten to a ragged stump, all the juicy little muscles bitten off and bones gnawed on.

As I panicked, things *shifted* overhead. Whatever was up there had rolled away a huge clump of earth to get at more of me. What else roamed the desert at night? Mountain lions. Bobcats. Coyotes. I could hear whatever it was industriously scraping away the dirt—if it got my elbow free before it started eating me, I was going to punch it.

Then, wave after wave of dirt began pouring away, sifting off. There was enough space that I could move—I wriggled up, fighting the earth itself to release me. I hauled myself out of the ground with a gasp, choking out the dirt that'd suffocated me. I took in long gulps of fresh, real, air. I was broken, I was starving, and there was blood— his blood.

The thing that'd freed me was a little feral wolf. Memories of being bitten rose hard and I wanted, *needed*, blood—and then I realized the smell of blood was coming from his paws. His claws were worn to nubs and he'd hurt himself, trying to rescue me.

118

I flopped down into the pit he'd dug and stared up at the night, waiting for my fangs to recede. He came up beside and snuffled me.

"Hey, Buster," I said, coming to my senses at long last. "I don't suppose you know what time it is."

He got his face in my face, looking down, and licked me.

We were far past the middle of the night and we were on the distant ass-cheek of civilization.

My healing abilities seemed to have given up on my whole ribs-lung issue, to concentrate on my ankle first, which was good because I could walk now—but every step I took made the rest of me hurt. The moon was out, nearly full, and with its light I could see the mess I'd made behind me—a large chunk of the desert looked slumped in, where the explosion had crushed the rest of the mine and bunker like a soda can, letting it fill in from the top down with rubble. Boulders had shifted and I couldn't make out anything of the trailer anymore, although could clearly see the plume of smoke drifting up from it, as could anyone else out tonight.

"We've got to get out of here," I told Buster. Rabbit seemed content to stay a wolf, and I was happy for him to be like that—it made traveling easier. Together, we staggered toward the nearest road.

Walking took an hour. I could feel the moon shifting overhead—if we were still exposed by dawn, I didn't know what I'd tell Rabbit to do. We were on the shoulder of a two lane road—Buster kept jogging off, doing wolf things, then coming back. I wondered what it felt like to be an animal in body, not just in spirit.

Just as I'd despaired of ever seeing a strip-mall again, headlights lit up the road ahead. I made my way out into the center of the road and waved my hands frantically. It was a late model Volvo and it slowed but the engine didn't stop.

"Accident—up ahead—need help," I said, clutching my side. I definitely still looked like a victim, and a thin coat of earth hid all of my tattoos. "Please."

I moved closer, blocking them, until I heard one of the windows roll down. "What?" asked a wary man with a European accent.

*"Turn off the car,"* I commanded, and he did so.

I SLID IN BESIDE HIM, and Buster hopped into the back. I didn't want to steal his ride, nor did I particularly want to drive. I directed him, while Buster paced back and forth in the back seat, looking out each window in turn. I hoped he wasn't leaving dusty wolfprints—I could make the driver pretty much forget everything else. I slumped against the window, watching the Volvo's clock count down. An hour before dawn, I had him pull into a business-park—it was the only safe place I could think of.

I got out, Buster leapt out, and I told the guy to forget everything and sent him on his way. And then I took Buster into the leafy bushes that flanked the business park's doors.

"You need to change back now, Buster."

Buster tilted his head at me. I knew he could hear me speaking, but did the words really make sense to him?

"I need to talk to Rabbit." I put my hand out, gesturing about how tall Rabbit was. Buster licked my palm, making that patch now the cleanest on my entire body. "Ugh," I protested, wiping my hand on my dirty jeans and—

With a strange unfurling, like the things that made Rabbit human were the petals of a carnivorous plant, the wolf tucked back inside, leaving a confused and naked little boy. He stood up, shaky. "What—happened?"

"You were a wolf again for a few hours."

"I was?" he asked, looking around, as if the night could prove it to him. "Why can't I remember anything?"

"I don't rightly know." I'd been worried about taking a wolf into Fran's—I hadn't really considered the alternative. But I needed to get somewhere safe to sleep, fast. I pulled off my shirt to give to him. "Come on, okay?" I said, putting my hand out. He took it, and we went to the front door together.

# CHAPTER FIFTEEN
## JACK

The bouncer to Francesa's sex club loomed before I could even ring. "Can I help you?" Vincent said, looking stern.

"Hey, Vincent," I said, trying to stand straight.

"Jack?" he guessed, like he didn't recognize me. "You look homeless."

"I feel homeless. I need Fran—can you get her for me?"

His wise face took in the way I looked—and the fact that I was holding the hand of a half-naked child, divided by the amount of time that Fran and I had been friends and the lengths that she'd gone to for me in the past. I knew I only barely came out ahead. "I can try. But you two'll have to wait over here," he said, drawing us in.

"We are *not* into that, Jack," Janice said, her eyes widening as Vincent directed us toward an open room right behind the check-in desk.

"Neither am I," I shouted back to her, just as Vincent closed the room's door on us.

It wasn't a broom closet, so there was that. But everything in it was velvet—I didn't feel comfortable standing in the room, much less sitting on any of the plush furniture, and Rabbit stood as close to me as he could without physically touching me.

"Where is this, Jack?" he asked, his voice small.

"Someplace safe," I said, hoping that Fran wouldn't turn me into a liar.

Fifteen minutes later, Fran burst in in full gear, a shining black latex bodysuit with a red harness atop it, crisscrossed everywhere a bikini would be. "I left a very important client in a very precarious situation to see to this, Jack," she said, taking me in, before looking over and finding Rabbit huddled behind me. "What. The…. I thought they were joking." Her eyes bore into me. "What on earth is this about?"

"We need someplace to hide, today." I could feel the dawn coming up.

She kept glaring. "Do I want to know why that child has no pants?"

"Not really. Trust me," I said, willing her to do so. "Come on, Fran. Don't you have a nursery set up for the diaper-people? Just hide us in a room where no one'll find us."

"Who's looking for you?" she demanded. "Because I'm out of," she began, ready to say blood, then went quiet for Rabbit's sake.

"Bad people," Rabbit said, from where he was hiding. Fran's eyebrows rose.

"I don't even need a full day—I just need till tonight. We didn't leave any tracks, and no one will expect to find us here, Fran."

"I need to know what I'm getting into, Jack." She looked leery and started shaking her head.

"What you're getting into is me owing you indefinitely after this. Weekly appointments. I'll let you schedule me, for real, like you've always wanted. Two hours."

Fran considered me, crossing her arms. The latex on her squeaked where it rubbed. "Eight."

"Three."

She squinted. "On weekends."

I could feel the weight of dawn, starting to press, and groaned. "Fine. But don't give us up to anyone. And he needs clothes."

"Yeah, he does," Fran started pacing. The soft red carpeting muted the clicks of her heels on the floor. "Okay." Fran squatted to get down onto Rabbit's level. "Hey. What's your name?"

"Rabbit," he said, from the vicinity of my thigh.

"I'm Fran." She put out her hand for Rabbit and he took it, shaking it quickly before hiding again.

I gave Rabbit's shoulder a squeeze. "Rabbit, I'm going to go to sleep soon—and Fran's going to take care of you, okay?"

Rabbit looked at Fran with his gray eyes. "Do you know any magic tricks?"

Fran blinked. "No."

Rabbit seemed relieved by that. "Good."

AFTER THAT, Fran procured very small women's clothes from Lord only knew where and soon Rabbit was in short-shorts and a crop-top, which was worse than than him swimming in my shirt if you asked me. But by then dawn was taking me down. Fran walked me to the broom closet and Janice had taken Rabbit down the hall. I knew being separated was the right thing to do, I knew he didn't need to see me die during the day, it'd only frighten him, but I couldn't help being worried about his next ten-or-so hours.

"Where are you taking him?"

"You're right, I do have a nursery. And no one's booked in it for a week. Not that you can stay here that long—and God help me if we do get raided, because a child in a nursery…."

"I just need absolute discretion until sundown."

"I can buy discretion. What I can't buy you is time. Is a day really going to cut it?" Fran unlocked the door to the closet—the lock was solid, and Fran made it clear she had the only key. It looked the same as when I'd left it, IV pole and all, and I stepped inside.

"I'm not sure. But I'll be able to come up with a better plan tomorrow night."

"And feeding?"

"I'll worry about that later."

Fran made a disgruntled noise but didn't press. "If I get any daytime trouble, we're handing him over. I'll hide him, but no one here is going to die for this."

"I wouldn't expect you to. And, again, I wouldn't bring him here if I didn't think it was safe."

"For him—or for us?" she asked, then raised both hands before I could answer her. "Don't. I get the feeling the more I know, the worse it's going to get. Just go lay down." She pointed to where I'd woken up the other night.

"I don't suppose...." I said, dancing the IV pole out of the way.

"I'm not holding out on you, if that's what you're asking."

I lowered myself to the ground. My hunger was hitting, hard. Dying would be a welcome respite—until I woke up again. "Anyone you can bleed during daytime?"

"Doubtful."

"Fair enough."

"More than fair." Fran took a big inhale—well, as big as she could, wearing what she was. "Good night, sweet prince."

"G'night, Francesca." I lay down, waving her off, and then crossed my arms over my chest ala Dracula, dramatically. I heard her laugh as she locked the door.

I wrestled with the dawn for as long as I could, and then it won.

# CHAPTER SIXTEEN
## ANGELA

*Just follow your nose,* felt like really trite advice, the further the truck rattled down the hill. But I'd never needed to sniff Rabbit out before—and I'd never been so free of silver. It was exhilarating—I found myself pushing the truck to the edge of its limits, going as fast as it could handle taking the turns, trusting my reaction-time utterly.

I slowed down as I was about to reach the real roads of civilization. If I got pulled over now, I'd be in trouble; I didn't have any ID and the truck wasn't mine. I hopped out, feeling the nearness of the moon over head, and breathed the desert air in deep.

*Rabbit, baby, where are you?*

Suddenly, there was the thinnest sliver of a scent I knew. Not the wildness behind me, the pine trees and the loam, or the dry dust ahead of me, with the scrub brush clinging on. But somehow I scented something familiar and known—even though I'd only had minutes with Rabbit after the magician had visited us earlier this night, before we had to say good-bye.

It didn't matter. His scent was written in my heart.

It smelled like home.

And he was out there, somewhere.

At a forty-five degree angle to the road. The truck couldn't go off road—but if I drove north eventually I'd find a turn.

I leapt back into the cab and rolled all the windows down.

AN HOUR OF DRIVING LATER, following roads I'd never been on before, my nose pulled me up to some kind of smoldering remains—with three motorcycles parked out front. *The Pack*—I turned off my headlights and coasted in in neutral, too late for safety, but I didn't care about that anymore. Had Rabbit been inside whatever structure that was? I parked and jumped out of the cab, running toward the fire, pulling my shirt in front of my face for protection. It was smoldering like an abandoned bonfire, and the scent of burnt plastic and over-heated metal combined into a tang that my shirt couldn't keep out.

"Rabbit? Rabbit!" I shouted, and then coughed. The bikes still had keys in their ignitions—and clothes set beside them as well, waiting for their owners to return. I shoved the first one over and all three fell like dominos, a thousand pounds of clanging chrome. "Rabbit!"

Nothing answered me. Not a shout—and not a howl.

Had he been inside that? I ran around the edges of it, calling out his name. He'd been here yes—I knew it, even through the scent of flames—but was he dead?

He couldn't be. I wouldn't accept that. Not now, not ever. I ran behind the hot heap and scrambled up the boulders behind it to look around, and saw where the earth was slumped, like someone had sucked it down from below with a straw.

Something bad had happened here. But Rabbit hadn't died...had he?

"Rabbit!" I shouted his name again, into the night. Nothing answered me except for miles of silence all around and the small hissing pops as the structure continued to cave in on itself.

Then a gust of wind blew up from the east, whipping the scents of chaos from my nose and mouth, replacing the heat and destruction with hard dry air and—a strangely familiar wolf.

My boy. My beautiful fur-covered baby. I took in a gulp of it, held my breath, and ran back to the truck.

AFTER THAT, I was afraid I lost the scent more times than I cared to admit. It came to me like morse code through the air, on-on-off, off-off-on. Any time I couldn't find it, I redoubled, daring to do circles in the road until I found it again to follow. I was reaching the end of a gas tank—another problem, seeing as I didn't have a credit card—when I pulled up in front of a non-descript office park.

The trail ended here, I could smell Rabbit—and Jack!—in the bushes near the entrance. Why, of all places, had Jack brought my boy here? I tried to look through the windows and couldn't, because of their tint and because of the glare of dawn. It was 9 AM and—of course. Since Jack was a vampire, his cultural bullshit was true too— just like I had to be a wolf on a full moon night, he had to sleep during the day. And if it was safe enough for him, it was safe enough for Rabbit.

I tried the door and found it locked. Then I started knocking.

A large bleary eyed man opened up the door a fraction of an inch. "We're closed."

"I need to come in. You have something of mine."

"There is no possible way that is true," he said, and moved to close it. I threw myself against it and we wrestled, each on our own side, both of us surprised by my strength. I got an elbow in, and as soon as I had the rest of the building for leverage it was over—he stepped back and I sagged forward.

"All right, you're in," he said, taking a step back. "What do you want?"

I was in a very posh waiting room, like for a very fancy spa, only most spas didn't have several hundred pound bouncers—or smell like sex. "My son is here somewhere."

One of his eyebrows rose high. "Are you, uh, one of them?" he asked, walking back behind the main counter.

"Depends on what you mean."

I saw his hand dive beneath the counter and realized there was a very real chance I was about to get shot. Then the curtains behind the desk flared open, revealing an oncoming woman in a robe, who'd been caught taking off her make-up. "Hello?" she asked, dramatically.

"I'm a friend of Jack's." I could still scent him in here, too, a little sweet, a little musky.

She looked me up and down and then shook her head wearily. "I figured. Come here," she said, waving me back.

We went through the curtains and down a long hall full of doors. Nothing about the situation made me feel safer, especially when the scent of sex—a lot of it, from a lot of people—still hung heavy in the air. So when instead of taking me to Rabbit, we went into a dressing room and she sat down, I stood near the door. "What's the meaning of this? Where's Rabbit?"

"Your boy's fine, I promise. But you and I need to have a heart to heart before I let you run off. It's Angela, isn't it?"

My eyes narrowed. "Yeah, it is."

"Well I'm Fran—and Jack's told me all about you." She held both her hands up and clawed her fingers, making the international thriller-sign for monster. Jack had...told her. "Don't look so dismayed. He's generally trustworthy—and I generally keep secrets."

And she, whoever she was, had been watching over my son since dawn. I perched on the seat across from her, trying to be polite.

"Thank you," she said, crossing her hands over one knee. "Now, what the hell is your plan?"

I blinked. "Excuse me?"

"Your plan. The resolution of all of this mess you're in."

I leaned forward in my chair. I would take this entire building apart to get to Rabbit if I had to. "If you know what I am, then you know what I can do—and I don't owe you anything," I snarled, letting a hint of my wolf through.

"You may not owe me—but your man's in a state."

My head whipped back. "Jack's not my man."

She pursed her lips and looked at me, as I felt a flush I couldn't control rise up. "All I am saying," she went on, sounding reasonable, "is that if you're running away—take your boy and go, and I'll clean up your mess somehow. But if you want to fight, Jack's going to want to be there. Only he's not in any condition at the moment."

"He...needs blood?"

She winced. "Something like that. So are you staying? Or are you going?"

I'd promised the wolves—and I wanted things done. "Till full moon night, yeah."

"And you want that foolhardy son-of-a-bitch to fight by your side?" She jerked her chin to wherever Jack was presumably sleeping.

"No!" I wouldn't let Jack fight my fights. He'd already done enough for me, keeping Rabbit safe from the Pack tonight. But... someone who understood the score needed to bear witness for me, and I couldn't imagine finishing things without him. "But I do want him there," I said, more softly.

"All right," Fran said. "Then I need to explain some strange things about vampires to you."

I leaned forward to listen.

RABBIT WAS CURLED INTO A BALL, sleeping in the corner of a room that looked like a nursery. I'd sworn not to ask any questions, which after seeing what he was wearing was hard. But he was so excited to see me, and I him—and I knew that he was fine. We'd made it through another storm somehow, he and I. I held him close and buried my face in his hair. He smelled different, ever since the magician had touched him, but he was still my boy.

"I'm so glad to see you, baby."

"Momma—you would not believe!" he started, then caught Fran listening in. He cupped his hands to my ear. "Buster's real, Mom. I'm a werewolf."

"I know, baby," I said, holding him tight.

He looked affronted, jaw dropped. "Why didn't you ever tell me?"

"I wanted you to be more grown up first. I didn't want you to fight your way out of things." I swallowed, and went for the full confession. "I'm one too."

His eyes went wide. "What about the bad people? Last night—" he began.

I hugged him until he stopped talking. "I want to hear your story, from the beginning to the end—but we need to get out of here, first."

"Okay," he said, and for once in his little boy life, didn't squirm to get free. He just quietly held me back.

I could've stayed there with him for hours, ignoring the creepy scenery, but—I looked back to Fran. "I don't have any money. And I'm almost out of gas."

"Don't worry, I'll just add it to Jack's tab." I had no idea what that meant, and I didn't want to—her smile was almost predatory.

I installed Rabbit in the truck, locked the doors, and walked back inside. Fran led me down a hallway and brought out a key that opened up a padlock as big as my palm.

"He's all yours," she said, sweeping the door open. A motion sensitive light turned on, and I saw Jack for the first time since leaving Mark's. He hardly looked like the same man.

I gasped. "Oh my God."

"Yeah. I've seen him dead before, but this is a little rough, even for him. He's totally safe right now, by the way," she said, wandering off to get something. I crept into the room. I smelled dirt, hell I saw it everywhere, poor Jack was covered in it, and his ribs were bent wrong, and some of his nails were missing. His boots were off, and one ankle was completely raw to where I thought I could see bone. "He's a tough motherfucker though. Don't let this fool you," Fran said, coming back in the room. She was holding a bolt of fabric. "Blackout curtains. Vegas's finest. I invest heavily." She thumped it on the ground beside him with a heave, and started stretching a fold out, while I stood, arms crossed, taking his wreckage in. She stopped and looked up at me. "I could use some help."

"Of course." I knelt down and stroked dirt out of his hair. Out of all the bosses he could've ever had—how on earth had he found me?

Fran cleared her throat. I flushed, and helped her roll him.

RABBIT and I drove to a run-down Target, a grocery store, and then to a sad hotel on the outside of town with its back to the desert. Jack was wrapped up in the truck's bed, with a zip tie on either end, and it made me nervous every time we left him that someone would want to get a closer look. Our luck held though, and no one was around to ask any questions when I slung him over my shoulder and took him inside the hotel, shoving him beneath the bed furthest away from the window. I got Rabbit in and out of a shower, took one myself, and then we both pulled on new outfits that smelled like the store, pulling the tags off with our teeth.

It turned out there wasn't much Rabbit could tell me, in between the PB&J's that I made him. He remembered a system of tunnels and some scary monster frightening him, meeting some vampires—a lady vampire who sounded suspiciously familiar, and I found my hand clenching tighter around my plastic knife—and then motorcycles coming. To think we'd still been sold out after all Mark's hard work—but Rabbit had been saved, due to Jack's equally quick thinking. Jack had practically thrown him out the door and shouted for him to run, so he did, for the boulders and then—he remembered nothing. Not until he'd turned back into a boy outside the bushes at Fran's this morning.

We lay together, snuggled tight after our makeshift meal. "So what happened to you, Mommy?"

I stared at the generic art hung high on one wall—probably to cover some prior guest's punch-hole. I could hear another couple fighting three doors down. "It's a long story. I met up with some werewolves, and then...."

"You got away? Was there fighting?"

"Yes and no. I got away. But—I made a promise that we'd go back."

"Back to them? But didn't they kill Grandma?" His little body tensed, and he growled. "We're going to kill the ones that killed grandma, aren't we."

"I don't know, baby. But we're going to try. It's the only way to get free." I'd bought a copy of the paper at the grocery store—Gray's escape had made the front page. Reading the headline had made the pit of my stomach drop like I'd taken another shot of silver. But it was all the more reason that we had to end this, somehow, someway.

"Momma can I watch cartoons?" Rabbit asked, as I stroked his hair away from his face.

"Sure, baby," I said, and handed the remote to him.

# CHAPTER SEVENTEEN
## JACK

I woke up from death to the sound of cartoons, in just as much pain and hunger as I had died. I worked my way free from folds of fabric and found myself staring up at the bottom of a mattress. I could smell Angela and Rabbit. They'd survived—*we'd all survived*.

I thumped my head against the floor behind me in relief. "There are definitely no dead hookers under here," I announced.

Both of them went still, and then Rabbit shrieked. "Jack!" and started peering underneath.

"Hey buddy," I said, reaching for the edge of the mattress to pull myself out. "I assume we're safe?" I was on the floor between two queen beds and eye level with a Book of Mormon.

Angela was smiling down gently. She looked goddamned beatific with the room's solo light on behind her, igniting each strand of her blond hair. "Yeah. We've got a day."

"And then what?"

"I'll explain in a bit," she said, tilting her head towards Rabbit.

"Sounds good." I folded my legs in, feeling the edges of my ribs grind as I stood. I knew I looked a sight now—how much worse had it been when I was dead? I wound an arm around my chest as a bolster, then staggered up to sit on the bed opposite them.

"I got you some new clothes," Angela said, standing and heading toward some shopping bags on the far side of the room.

"And I'll make you a sandwich!" Rabbit announced. He was jumping on the bed, and the thing inside me that was always hungry, watched him—even as Angela, now frozen, was looking over her shoulder, watching me.

"Thanks," I told him, forcing myself to look away. "Can I shower?"

"Please," Angela said, gesturing toward the back of the room.

I WENT into the bathroom and got the full view. I was covered in dirt and my chest was dented. I couldn't eat, but I could at least get clean. I reached in to start the shower, and then moved to unbuckle my pants as the door opened behind me. I whirled.

Angela was there, holding out a bag of clothing and Tupperware container of something red and sloshy. "I got you this."

I took it from her and opened it up. Pig's blood. Congealed. My fangs didn't throb. Drinking it would be like drinking phlegm. "Thanks, but no thanks," I said, pouring the contents down the shower drain. "Fran talked to you, I assume?"

"Yeah. She gave me some money, too. Said she'd add it to your tab."

I snorted. "I'll bet."

Standing there, half-naked, I could almost feel her watching me. It would be so easy to do half-a-hundred things to her, and my hunger thought she would be as delicious as the pig's blood was disgusting. "I've never seen all your tattoos before," she said.

"Well you're still up on me." I forced a smile.

She closed the door behind herself and leaned into it. "I know you've got to feed, Jack."

"I can go another day." I took a step away from her, and found myself trapped by the bathroom's back wall. The thought of her offering made my heart both thrill and sink. I wanted her, badly, I always had—but didn't want to be anyone's pity case, least of all hers.

"You look like hell."

"Just let me shower," I said gruffly, concentrating on the task at hand. I shoved my jeans the rest of the way off and got into the shower, hauling the curtains closed around me. I stood in the stream and watched dirt wash away, until I heard the bathroom door close.

WHEN I CAME OUT, Rabbit had my PB&J ready. I took it and stationed myself on the bed nearest the window. If anyone came, they'd have to deal with me first.

I ate the sandwich, for all the good it'd do, and saw Rabbit trying to hide a grin. "What?"

"You look like a lost golfer."

"Rabbit," Angela chided, then flushed. "I'm sorry, I was shopping quickly."

I plucked at the light colored jeans she'd picked out. Between those, the green polo shirt, and what I would charitably decide to call 'salmon'-colored Vans sneakers, he was right. "So I figured. Thanks."

"You're welcome."

I lay back on the bed, listening in between cartoons to the sounds outside. Angela didn't seem like she was in a rush to leave. But the longer we stayed here, the more of the night we wasted. Eventually I sat up. "Hey, Rabbit, can you do me a favor?"

"Yeah," he said, sitting cross legged up at the front of their mattress, eyes on the TV.

*"Go to sleep,"* I said, and he did, immediately. He would've fallen

onto his head had both Angela and I not raced to catch him. I got there first, but I let her take him from me.

"So you can do that too?" she said, holding him across her body like a pieta statue.

"Yeah. I can undo it if you want—but we need to talk."

"Because you're hungry?" she asked, her eyebrows furrowing in concern.

"Of course I am. But I'm more interested in knowing what your plan is. Just sitting here, watching TV doesn't feel like one." I went to safely sit back on the other bed. "After your car pulled away from Mark's garage—what happened to you?"

She carried Rabbit back and pushed the sheets down on their bed to tuck him in, and then sat on its corner, matching me, so that we were on separate queen-bed islands. I kicked off the horrible pink shoes to tuck one leg up under me, ignoring the way my wolf-chewed ankle felt raw.

"I found my people, Jack. For the first time—and they taught me what it meant to be a wolf. Some of them sprung Gray from jail—but others gave me that truck outside." She straightened her shoulders, preparing to tell me a fact, I could tell. "I'm going back with Rabbit tomorrow night."

"What?" I almost shouted. Luckily, I didn't have to worry about waking Rabbit. "That's insane!" I hissed more quietly.

"I have to finish this, Jack. I've been running from it long enough."

"So, what? We're just going to take on an entire pack of wolves?" When three of them the night prior had almost killed me?

"No—I just want you there for a witness. To take word back to Mark. The actual fight is just going to be mine."

I groaned. "That's even more insane."

"It's not," she said, shaking her head quickly. "I think some of them will have my back."

"You made...friends?" I asked carefully.

"Yeah, I did." Her eyes went distant, thinking about it, and I felt like I could almost see the wolf inside of her, before she blinked herself back to the present. "Hey—I met a Jonah. You wanted to tell me something about him—what was it?"

My hand rose, to touch the spot on my chest where Bella's planchette had burned me, until I'd buried it in Tamo's eye. "Yeah—he was a friend of a pregnant friend of mine who was murdered."

Angela's whole body went tense. "Murdered? You're sure? She didn't just miscarry in a messy way?"

"I saw the crime scene. I'd slept with her the night before. She begged me to stay with her, because she was worried about a fight but...." I shrugged one shoulder helplessly. "I couldn't. I had to get back to work, and then home to die. It was the same night Dark Ink's windows broke." I sighed, remembering the loss of Bella all over again. "Paco's got police connections. He found out she was going to have a boy."

Angela's jaw dropped. "I've got to tell Jonah. Once he hears that —once they *all* hear that—I think it'll change the tide."

I gave her a disbelieving look, and knew she was still considering her options with the Pack. "And he'll just trust you? That's how wolves work?"

"Wolves don't lie," she murmured.

I pondered this a moment. "I guess a vampire isn't like a wolf then."

She stopped thinking then and looked up, reaching out for me. "You've never lied to me, Jack. Lies of omission, sure, but never when it counted."

I gave the mattress a hangdog smile and did not take her hand. "Shows what you know. I lied to you in the bathroom just now." I couldn't go another day. Not like this. I'd be a danger to everyone when I woke up again. I couldn't play chicken with their lives based on my pride. I got up off the bed and pulled the first of the ridiculous shoes back on. "I'll be back."

"No," she protested.

"I have to, Angela. It's what I am, I'm sorry." I couldn't meet her gaze, I just pulled the heel of the second shoe up.

"I mean you don't have to leave to do that. My offer's still good." I heard her get up off the mattress, and knew she was coming around.

"You need to fight."

"Not till tomorrow. I hear I heal pretty fast." She ducked her head so that I had no choice but to see her.

"It's not like I'm going to go kill some hobo—I won't drink too much, and I'll make them forget they ever saw me."

"Or, you could drink from a friend," she said, putting a hand against my jaw. Her touch didn't shock me anymore, but the need that flowed through me was a thousand times more profound.

"You're sure?" I heard myself ask, as what blood I did have fell south.

"Wolves don't lie," she said again and turned, walking back into the bathroom. I waited half a second, and then followed her.

"I don't want Rabbit to see," she said, closing the door behind me. There was no way in the small space for her to not rub up against me as she did so. Inside me, the hunger rose up, slavered, and grew wings.

"He'll sleep until morning, or until I tell him to wake up," I told her, watching her, embarrassed by how eager I was, hoping she couldn't tell.

"Well," she announced, giving me a brave smile. "How does this go?"

Half the bathroom was mirror, half the bathroom tile. "I guess it depends—do you want to see?" I'd get to see her transform tomorrow night—letting her watch me bite her if she wanted seemed only fair.

She nodded slowly. "Yeah, I do."

"All right then." I grabbed her gently by the shoulders and turned her toward the mirrors, standing behind her. She smelled good, like shampoo and soap; whatever the magician had done hadn't changed her base scent by more than a note or two.

"Jack?" she asked, and I opened up my eyes. I hadn't realized they were closed, as I was stroking my face through her hair.

"Sorry," I apologized, stepping back. She'd offered blood and nothing more. I popped the polo's collar. "This is totally how Bella Lugosi would've wanted it," I said. She laughed, and I engulfed her, without thinking. One arm around her body, the other pulling her head to one side by her chin. "Don't fight, don't fight, don't fight," I whispered, before my fangs made speech impossible. Her hands grabbed mine in terror, wrestling me as I wrestled with my hunger. It wanted—*oh the things it wanted*—but she was *mine*, she'd offered herself to *me*, not it, and I wouldn't hurt her any more than I had to. I breathed a warning, and then my sharp fangs pierced her sweet pale skin. She gasped, went still, and blood welled up inside the wounds. I moved to lap at it, holding her close, swaying to her blood's time, like we were in a profane dance. Such hot, sweet, softness, rolling over my tongue, so easy to get lost in. I could feel it healing me, giving me everything I needed....

One trembling hand rose up to touch my face. Angela combed her fingers through my hair and broke the spell. I made my fangs retract, even as my hunger cried, it could've taken so much more. I slowly released her, both of us leaning forward against the sink. She twisted her head to inspect where I'd bitten her.

"Did you get enough?" she asked, panting.

There was no way she couldn't feel the hard-on I had—I hastily backed up. "Yeah," I lied.

"Really?"

I lifted the bottom of the polo, and showed her where my chest was whole, ribs back where they belonged.

"Good," she said, touching her neck with fluttering fingers.

"I'm sorry if I scared you. I didn't mean to, I just—"

"Shh. Don't apologize." She turned and put fingers on my lips to silence me. "We're monsters. That's the way we are."

"Yeah," I agreed, and retreated to the other room.

# CHAPTER EIGHTEEN
## ANGELA

I crawled into bed beside Rabbit while Jack went back to being lonely, sprawled out on his bed, staring up at the ceiling. To think, all those years I'd thought that I was an island, and I'd never seen the other one floating right beside me.

Before I could say anything profound, he sprang up out of bed. "I'm going to go take a walk. Check the perimeter and all that."

My wolf was restless inside, it was like she was pacing—I didn't think I'd sleep tonight, or tomorrow. "Want some company?"

He paused, considering, then answered slowly. "Sure."

I wrapped up in a coat and we both stepped outside, where I set all the locks. The hotel was an L-shape, with an alcove full of benches and vending machines at the corner, and we walked its longest edge. The parking lot was empty, except for the car I assumed belonged to that other couple—they'd stopped fighting about an hour ago. Across that was a two way street, and then rolling desert beyond. I could feel my wolf's urge to go run in it underneath the waxing moon, matched only by her desire to stay here, close to Jack. Getting bitten had startled her, but also cemented some part of her interest in him. He was dangerous and still, somehow, safe.

"Aren't you cold?" I asked him. A conversation would keep my feelings human.

"No. Your blood's pretty warm."

"You're welcome," I said, leaning over to nudge him. He seemed surprised by that, taken aback almost. "How many people know?"

"Three-ish, now that there's you. That's not including other vampires, obviously."

I grinned. "Wow, I'm a member of a very elite group."

"Just don't go comparing notes on me." He kept watching me out of the corner of his eyes. "And, obviously, don't go telling anyone."

"I won't. I just can't believe I didn't figure it out. All those years you worked for me...." I let my voice drift and laughed. "Here I thought that I was lucky that you were willing to work nights—until I realized how good you were and got pissed that you wouldn't work days, to make both of us more money."

"Yeah, well, day shift was never in the cards for me, sorry." He gave me a sheepish grin.

I stopped just outside of a halo of streetlight. "And all that time you never guessed about me?"

Jack shrugged. "You were always masked by the silver. And I guessed that you were stressed, being a single mom and all." He blew air through his pursed lips. "I always wanted to help you more, Angela, but really the only way I could do that was by being a good employee. Which I did try to do."

My eyebrows crawled up my forehead. "In between sneaking out to sleep with people," I said. "Or, sleeping in-house, with clients."

He gave me one of his wicked grins. "I can't help it if I'm personally responsible for most of our fantastic Yelp ratings. I just never let a customer leave unhappy." I rolled my eyes at him and he laughed, as he went on. "But no, I never guessed. I didn't even know werewolves existed, until I started trying to figure out who killed Bella."

"Jonah's girl. Who...it sounds like you were also sleeping with?" I don't know why I bothered to make it sound like a question.

He winced a little. "I slept with her first, if that makes it better." He inhaled deeply and shrugged. "I sleep with a lot of people."

And oddly, around me, he seemed shy of that fact. "So I've heard," I teased.

It was his turn to roll his eyes. "Fran," he said with a groan, and I laughed.

"I didn't need Fran to tell me that. A guy who looks like you? Single? In Vegas? Please." And just how many times had I imagined sleeping with him? Even when I was on silver? I rose up on my toes and then settled back down.

"All right, fine. I keep busy," he said, shrugging again. "But it's not like something I'm proud of."

That was the first time I'd ever heard contrition in his voice. "Why not?"

"Because this isn't how I want to be." He put his hands in his jeans pockets and looked out at the desert behind me. "It's like I'm always starving. Sometimes that's okay because the world's the biggest buffet ever. But then other times I find something that I know is going to taste better than anything else, and I realize if I let myself go I might eat it all up, and I'll never be able to taste it again. Everything I'm actually hungry for shouldn't be around me." He looked down and caught me watching him. "It's not a good metaphor," he said, with a headshake.

"No—I know exactly how that feels." Like spending seven years waiting for the Pack to find me, afraid every day in the meantime.

"Maybe you do," he acknowledged with a nod.

The streetlight cast him in stark relief, one half of him flooded with light, the other shadowed completely, turning his profile into a rising moon. His hair hung loose, without product at long last, and the dragon tattoos on his arms were in direct opposition to the polo I'd bought him too quickly this morning.

He'd had always been available at the shop, and even though he was polite and never pressed, I'd always known it. I'd kept the knowledge of his interest in my back pocket for years, for whenever I was down. Any time that I'd thought that I was too much or too diffi-cult for any man to handle, I'd always known that Jack wasn't afraid of the hassle of me. I had known him, trusted him, for so long, and here we were beneath the open sky.

"So what's it like being a werewolf?" he said, and broke the spell, turning to walk up the L's short-side.

"I don't know. I haven't been one very long." I trotted after him.

"Rabbit seemed to get the hang of it fast."

"Yeah, well, he's young. He's always liked his wolf—I've always been afraid of mine."

"Why?"

"It's hard to explain. She's wild. And I'm not used to being a democracy—she has her own opinions."

Jack chuckled. "Yeah? Like what?"

"Like…." I started to say, and then the moment went on too long, and he turned to look at me fully, waiting. "She likes you," I breathed.

He was silent, and then said, "But you love Mark." I nodded, as he took a long inhale. "I can see how that would be awkward."

"It is," I admitted. "Especially because she's not wrong to like you."

One of his eyebrows quirked up. "So how many votes does she get?"

"Just one. Same as me."

"And how do you break ties?"

"There's no need." I stepped forward and leaned up, knowing he would meet me there.

His lips met mine just as I knew they would, but everything else was chaste—he didn't reach for me—and he didn't press his tongue in. He pulled back, staring down. "I don't want you to do anything you'll regret, Angela."

"It's far too late for that, Jack. I might die tomorrow night. I don't want to die alone."

His dark eyes searched mine, and then he physically picked me up, carrying me towards the alcove.

MY ARMS WRAPPED around his neck instinctively as he planted me against the hotel's cinderblock wall.

"I've wanted this for so long," he whispered, brushing hair out of my face. I felt my wolf rush forward, and fought her down. She could enjoy this from the backseat, but I wanted to be fully human for these last few memories.

"Me too," I whispered back. His forehead was pressed against mine, our breaths intermingled, and I wanted him to kiss me.

As if knowing that, he leaned in. Our lips met, parted, and our tongues pushed, needing to taste each other at last. My hands raced to touch him, anywhere I could get. Everything I'd been denying myself for years I wanted, all at once, right now—and I knew he felt the same. I could feel it up and down his body—the way his teeth pulled at my lips when he leaned back, the way his hands stroked at my chest, my waist, the way I could feel his hard-on straining against my thigh.

He pulled back and started kissing my throat and neck as if he were going to devour me, and I wound one hand into his hair, clawing the other one up his back, and I started making quiet sounds.

"Please," he asked for permission a second before he did it anyways, pulling my shirt up and out, falling to a crouch in front of me, hands pushing up my bra. His hot mouth trailed against my stomach and I didn't know which way to beg, to pull him up or push him down. One hand stroked a breast as the other pushed up my skirt. His mouth found my other nipple and—I was pinned against the wall as he licked at me, tugged at me, and started to softly finger the outside of my pussy through the fabric of my underwear.

"God, Jack," I'd been overwhelmed before, but not like this, his need was like a tidal wave, sucking me down.

He rose back up to kiss me again, leaving his hand where it was between my legs, not pushing in, warming me up, torturing me. "The entire time I've known you, Angela—all the nights I dreamed I was with you when I was with other women," he said, the words muffled in between kisses against my neck. "All the times I wanted to touch you, to taste you—every day knowing that I shouldn't." He licked his tongue up from my collarbone to my ear, and he shifted the fabric barrier protecting me aside, and started touching between my legs, skin to skin. "Afraid of showing you what I was—of you ever finding out how hungry you made me."

I grabbed his head and brought his mouth to mine, kissing him hard. "Do you think you were the only one?" I whispered.

"I didn't dare to hope," he whispered back—and pushed his fingers inside me.

I cried out, and then kissed him again as I tilted my hips toward his hand. His body was pressed against mine—but I wanted more—I started raking his shirt up—I wanted to touch more of him, needed more of him touching me—as his fingers pushed deeper and his palm began to grind.

He pulled out of me and back for a moment, to take off his shirt and cast it aside. I reached to feel his skin—kissing his chest as his arms rose around me to shove my coat back and down. The night air flooded us both, but I wasn't cold anymore—I belonged in it.

"Angela," he said, catching my chin and pulling me up. "I'm not going to let you die tomorrow."

"Dying's not the plan. It's just a possibility." I finished pulling my coat off, throwing it toward his shirt. "And you're still going to be asleep at moonrise. So you don't get a choice." He knew it was true as I said it, and I watched his expression crumple in agony. "Shh—it's okay, Jack."

"But there's got to be a—"

"No," I interrupted. "No suggestions. I'm over all of that. No more money, no more time. I need things to be done." I rested one hand on his chest, over his heart and the head of a dragon tattoo. "That's why I need this, now, please," I said quietly.

The way he looked at me then, so full of meaning and intent—I would've swayed, were I not against a wall. "Okay," he said, and it sounded like a promise.

We kissed again then, like both of us were fragile things, holding one another's faces, tasting gently, pulling softly, moving as one, the flashfire of earlier passion quenched, with something hotter and deeper building in its place. He pulled back, studying me again, and then lowered himself, grabbing hold of my shirt and pulling it up again, rubbing his face between my breasts before he kissed them all over, one by one, as I rested my hands on his shoulders and leaned back, looking down, wanting to watch him to take his fill of me, making small sounds as each kiss, lick, and caress, stoked heat inside my hips.

As his mouth started to move down my stomach I knew where this was leading—and reached down to pull my skirt up, as his hands rose underneath, stroking up my thighs. His fingers caught the edges of my underwear and tugged, pulling them down for me to step out of, then his eyes on me all the while his mouth went—there —kissing my pussy, tonguing my clit. I made another sound of submission and pushed my hips off the wall, offering everything to him, and felt him purr against me.

His mouth—God, *his mouth*—he sucked and pulled and his lips were strong except for when they needed to be soft and his tongue rolled against me, riding under my hood, teasing my clit out, as his chin ground up and in. Both of his hands had moved to cup my ass, as my hands found his hair, to make sure he followed as my hips started to rock—and then he pulled back, and reached one hand up, bringing his first two fingers up between my thighs to slide them inside.

"Yeah—yes," I breathed, as he started pulsing them in and out of me.

"You taste so good, Angela," he whispered, looking up, watching the mess he was making of me. He reached up with his other hand for my breast—and then fastened his mouth back onto my clit as I moaned.

His hand, his mouth, his fingers—I never knew which one I liked best—the sharp sensation of a nipple being pulled, or the way his tongue worked my clit making everything hot, or how his fingers now were settled deep inside me, no longer pounding but rubbing, as if my orgasm were a thing that needed to be coaxed.

My hips rocked and thrust, my body thrashed, I rose up on my toes and shouted. The sound of me coming echoed in the small space, each reverberation pulsing as I did, my pussy clenching, my hips bucking, one hand clawed into his hair, the other scrabbling for purchase on the wall. Jack kept his mouth against me, kissing and sucking, determined to see me through until the very end—I looked down and saw him looking up, knew he was waiting on me, like he always had. I put a thigh over his shoulder and pushed his head toward it. "Drink," I whispered hoarsely.

He did.

# CHAPTER NINETEEN
## ANGELA

How could I not taste Angela when she wanted me to? The life she'd given me—the orgasm she'd had, had released us both. It was like we'd been carrying a heavy weight for so long we didn't even remember why we'd been holding it anymore. Feeling her life wash over me, it was like an uncorking of possibilities, for both of us—and then her leg on my shoulder and her hands insisting?

No vampire could resist.

I pressed her back against the wall first and took my time, licking her, kissing her. I knew the exact place I would sink my fangs, the exact duration I would drink from her for, already salivating at the way her blood would taste—I put a hand beneath her knee, held her ready, and—my fangs slid out, straight into her soft flesh. She gasped, her body tensed, but her hand in my hair didn't try to push me away—instead it pulled me towards her, burying my face in her thigh the way it'd just been on her pussy.

She wanted me to have this. Knowing what I was. Unafraid. Her blood siphoned into me and it felt like fire coursing through my veins. I pulled back, barely, mouth agape with still hungry fangs, panting against her as they receded, unable to remember the last time I'd felt this alive.

Alive—and I needed someone else to feel it too. I looked up and saw her looking down, disheveled and panting. She slid down the wall to straddle me—and her lips met mine, surely tasting her blood and juices on me, as her hands dove between her thighs to catch at my jeans, where my hard-on was straining.

"God—yes." I rose up, kissing her, finding her hands with my own, shoving my jeans down far enough to free my cock, before capturing her in my arms and twisting us both to the ground, gently placing her on her coat. "I need to be inside you," I warned, as her hands caught my face to kiss me again, and her hips tilting up in permission. I kissed her, and then I rose up on both my arms, to watch her face the moment I pushed in.

She released a soft gasp and her jaw dropped and then she made a soft whine as I slid deep, her pussy slick and tight. I'd imagined this so often—but the reality was better than I could've dreamed. I pulled back, and thrust again, just feeling the heat of her envelope me. Her feet kicked up and looped around my back, as I leaned in, burying myself inside her.

"Oh, Angela," I whispered, as I started up a rhythm.

"I know," she said, kissing at my jaw and neck. "I know."

I cradled her head in my hands, trying to keep it from the hard cement, as her hands wandered up and down my back and our hips joined, mated, rocking together as one. I'd needed this—*for so long*— her body yielding beneath me, her blood coursing through my veins, the way her pussy held me, the ever-quicker soft sounds she made.

"Jack," she said, looking up at me, helplessly, ready to give herself over so soon again. "Jack—don't stop—Jack—don't ever stop."

"I won't," I swore, lifting her to me as my hips thrust in—and I got to feel her come again, as she cried out, her body rocking against mine, her pussy pulsing around me, another wave of life spilling out —it only served to make me harder. I paused over her, taking it in, breathing deep, as she relaxed back with a moan.

"Oh—Jack," she said, looking up. Her eyes were wild—I wondered if I was seeing her wolf come through. "That's so good."

"Yeah?" I asked, with a thrust.

"Yeah," she said, placing her feet back beside me to thrust up.

"I don't want to wear you out," I said, which was a complete lie and maybe the stupidest thing I'd ever said in my life.

She gave me a wicked grin. "I don't think that's possible."

"Good," I said, grabbing her wrists and hoisting them high. She fought back—and I realized I'd forgotten how strong werewolves could be. I pushed her back down, only barely winning. "So it's going to be like that, is it?"

Her eyes searched mine. "Until you fuck me, yes."

And just when I thought there was nothing in the world that could've made me harder—I successfully caught her wrists in one hand and then her face with the other and kissed her hard, while I thrust.

Before that moment, we'd been the humans we always pretended to be. After that, though—we became what we were. I pounded into her, my cock desperate to feel the friction of each hot stroke while she raised her hips for me, grinding her clit against me each time. Our kisses became savage, and our hands—I let go of hers, and she used them to claw at me, translating our fucking into marks down my back, as I wound one hand into her hair to hold her still, like a predator paralyzing prey. I wanted her to know that I was in control, even as I wanted her to want me—

"God—Jack," she warned, but she didn't have to, I felt it too, the way she was ready, how she wanted to be conquered, and I wanted to bury my cock so far inside.

"Fucking come for me, Angela," I growled—and she did.

This orgasm was like a roman candle firework, huge, pulsing, waves, that demanded that I come *now*. I grunted and thrust and felt my balls lifting, spilling myself inside her, finally giving her back some of the life that she'd given to me. "Yes," I said low, pounding myself in. "Yes—yes—yes," I grunted with each thrust until I finished. I collapsed on top of her, both of us sweaty despite the night air. She pulled my head down, and stroked her fingers through my hair and down my back, where they traced over the welts they'd left behind.

"I didn't know it could be like that," she said to herself. "Did you?"

I moved to kiss her collarbone. "I'd hoped." What were we now? Had anything changed?

Neither one of us made to move—neither one of us wanted this to end. If a car had driven up, or if we'd heard anything, we would've stopped, I knew—but since we hadn't—I twisted my head down, to kiss across the dark roses on her chest and take her breast back into my mouth.

She moaned, low and long, as I flicked her nipple with my tongue. She gently tapped the back of my head, as if for my attention, and she had it. "I have an odd request," she asked, as I lifted my head up.

I chuckled. "You have no idea the things I've done. Ask it."

"You know how I said my wolf gets a vote?"

I lifted my head up even further. "I'm not having sex with a wolf."

Angela laughed. "She...won't be a wolf. She'll just be me. In my body. I—she—won't be able to talk...and I won't remember what she's done. Not all the way."

"I'm not in—" I started, to tell her I wasn't in love with her wolf. I caught myself, too late to deny it, and felt myself flush. "I'm not interested in you because of your wolf."

"I know that. But she's interested in you." If Angela realized what I'd almost said, she had the kindness not to let on. "She thinks you're manly or something."

"Hmm," I said, nuzzling against her breast.

"Not manly—wolf-ly," Angela informed me, after some internal conference. "Like you're some sort of big bad wolf—even though I keep telling her you're not."

"She's not wrong," I said. I went still for a moment though, remembering Bella's appraisal of me. "Let her out."

Angela nodded, and then closed her eyes. I could feel her body tensing in strange ways beneath me and then—opening her eyes again, she lifted her head to look back down.

The thing that was inside her now wasn't human. I backed up to kneel as she gathered herself, taking our surroundings, and then me, in. She stayed crouched in a way that would've made a human ache, and leaned forward, breathing me. I stayed completely still, while watching her. What could she—this thing that'd been hiding in Angela, punished by silver this whole time—possibly know about me?

I brought a hand up, and she took it in her teeth, holding it as she moved to be on all fours. She let go and turned, so that I was now behind her—where for the first time I saw all of Angela's tattoos.

"Oh," I breathed, stroking along her back without thinking. She was covered in a full English garden, riotous greens and blooms, with a little sleeping rabbit nestled at the center. I leaned in, and traced the artwork with one hand. Who had given her these? What I would've done to get the chance to draw on her perfect skin....

Angela's wolf looked over her shoulder at me, eyes alien. She licked her lips, and whined.

"You think I'm a wolf?" I asked her. Everything about her body tensed into attention. "You think you know more about me than I do? Why?"

She knelt a little, sending Angela's bottom back. The screen of her skirt rubbed against me—and the thought of being inside her again made me hard. I knew she'd still be wet, between all her orgasms and the load I'd put in her—Angela's wolf gnashed her teeth at me, and then fell to her elbows on the ground, offering me Angela's perfect ass.

I swatted it, sitting back down.

"Sorry, wolf-thing. Can you bring Angela back, please?"

Angela's wolf looked over her shoulder at me, abashed, and then sank to the ground, closing her eyes—and the Angela I knew returned. "How long's it been? What'd I miss?"

"Almost nothing. I couldn't do it."

"A request too odd for you even, eh?"

"Sorry," I said. "Your wolf isn't you." Just like I prayed my hunger wasn't really me.

"It's okay," she said, sitting back.

"So...what now?" I asked, unwilling to try to define tonight on my own.

"I don't know. She's all hot and bothered and," she moved to be on her hands and knees looking over her shoulder again. "She'll still take what she can get of you. And—so will I."

The look she gave me then—I lifted her skirt, and mounted her quickly, sliding deep back inside.

# CHAPTER TWENTY
## JACK

I took her wildly, because I knew that she could take it, and because I needed to—and I knew from the low moans she made as my cock bottomed out inside her that she needed it, too. She splayed her fingers on the ground and shoved her ass back for me—I reached down and spread her cheeks wide so I could see myself enter her with each thrust, wrapped around me, stretched tight.

"*Fuck, Jack*," she hissed my name and her elbows softened, as though I'd hit a switch somewhere inside her, making her collapse forward, creating a cradle with her arms for her head as she offered everything to me. "Just—*fuck*."

"I am," I growled a promise, relishing every sensation with each thrust. I slowed, panting. I couldn't give her anything but tonight—even if we lived, I had no illusions, I knew that she'd go back to Mark.

But for the length of tonight...she was mine.

I ran my hands up her sides slowly.

"What're you doing?" she dreamily asked.

"Deciding."

Her eyes fluttered open. "On what?"

My cock had already been painted with her wetness and my cum, but I realized I wanted more memories than that—if I lived past tomorrow night, I wanted to be able to close my eyes and bring up this moment forever: Angela bowed down in front of me, only barely balanced, working on my cock with her tongue and her lips.

"On this," I told her. "Turn around, Angela." She blinked, slowly coming to attention as I pulled my cock out of her. Its glistening length bobbed between us, already missing the sleeve of her cunt. "I'm going to fuck you every which way." I put my hand out for her as she got on all fours and turned toward me, sensing my need. She ran her cheek against my palm so that my fingers tangled in her hair. "Yeah," I whispered, taking hold of it, bringing her kiss-swollen lips to the head of my cock. Her eyes flashed up at me, not in defiance, but in genuflection, and I shuddered, right down to the bottom of the soul I knew I didn't have, as her tongue took its first taste.

She licked up the length of my shaft, as though she was trying to clean off the mess we'd made earlier. She took long eager stripes that made me ache, while looking up at me through blond eyelashes, like some sort of semi-innocent angel that I was perverting. I grabbed the base of my cock and tilted it forward for her with meaning, making a primal sound.

She laughed and wrapped her lips around me at last, innocence forgotten, and started sucking, wrapping my shaft with one hand, slicked with her spit, working me like a pro. I rocked my head back, giving into the moment, relishing each sensation: the way the back of her throat made me bend and rub, her tongue soft against my hardness, and the way she started moaning with each stroke.

She pulled off and held me with two hands to catch her breath, rubbing her tongue up and down my tip, licking off the precum there as fast as it was beading. "You like that?" she asked, and I was about to answer with something casual and snarky when I realized that she meant it.

All she wanted to do in this very moment was to please me.

It broke my heart, and then it put it back together again.

"Yes," I whispered, and she nodded, then went back at it, plunging me into her throat as I swung my hips up, I couldn't help it. If she wanted to make me happy, then I was going to have to let her. I slid my fingers into her hair again, and felt her nod permission as I began to thrust, fucking her mouth, slowly at first, and then faster once I realized she could take it—and that she wanted to be taken.

*By me.*

"Fuck, Angela," I groaned. She purred around me and made an accommodating whine as she gave up on stroking me, moving to hold herself up, while I used her mouth and lips and everything else, rocking into her, again, and again, unable to get enough, and then I felt her hand reach up and stroke my sack, like she wanted what was in it.

"Yeah," I growled. I didn't ask her if she cared that I come in her mouth because I already knew the answer. "You're gonna get it. But don't swallow."

She made a small questioning sound, but didn't stop, and at that trusting obedience after everything else that'd come before, I came, *oh God, I came*, so hard and long, pouring into her, my orgasm prolonged by knowing just how I was going to fill her next.

I took hold of the base of my cock again as she pulled off of it, sucking up every drop, and then looked at me, cheeks flushed and lips red. Blood was soaring inside of her, it was like I could see her arousal written on her, just beneath her skin.

I held my free hand out, making a cup of it just below her lips. "Spit."

Her eyes went wide, but she did was she was told, indelicately letting my load fall into my palm. She gave me a guilty look and a dazed smile. "What, is it poisonous to werewolves?"

"No," I told her, my voice low and serious. "The opposite in fact. Turn around."

Her eyes nervously ran across my face, but then she moved to do as she was told, looking over her shoulder at me once more. "Jack," she said, making my name a soft question.

"Every which way," I reminded her. "If you'll let me."

Her jaw dropped a little in surprise, but then she nodded again, and I used my cum and her spit to slick her asshole.

# CHAPTER TWENTY-ONE
## JACK

I was hard in an instant—I hadn't stopped being hard after fucking her mouth, once I'd realized this was next and was almost certain that she'd let me. I rubbed the rim of her asshole with my wet thumb and heard her moan, "Oh, God."

That was my cue. I came up close behind her and pulled my cock up through her dripping pussy, and then set it where it belonged, the last place on her that I needed to know—that I couldn't go through the rest of my hopefully long life without knowing.

I reached down and moved one of her knees out, sending her lower, and then I bent over her, supporting myself on one hand, as I used the other to steady my slow slide in.

Angela twisted her head back to look at me and I caught her lips in a deep kiss. I loved feeling her pant and tense against me, knowing I was stretching her wide, but also knowing that she could handle it, because right now she was mine. I rocked my head back even as I kept pushing in, taking her lower lip with me, dragging it between my teeth, watching her eyes go half-lidded and feeling her shudder.

I let go of my cock and wrapped her with my arm, holding her against me as I pushed myself deep, until I landed inside her ass as far as I could go. "Oh Angela," I breathed against the veil of her hair. She nodded quickly and started to wriggle, begging to be taken, sinking a hand between her thighs.

"I just...," she started without finishing.

"I know," I answered her, biting against her shoulder with human teeth, and rose up to start to thrust.

I NEVER PULLED out of her all the way, just up until the point where the ridged head of my cock caught the rim of her ass and tugged. She was so tight, and it felt so good, but I didn't want to ever leave her.

She slowly lowered herself down, one bent arm braced against the ground, her cheek against her coat, calling my name softly with each of my strokes, "Jack, Jack, Jack."

"You like that?" I asked her, every bit as solemn as when she had asked me.

"Yeah," she said, just as truthful as I had been, as she nodded and pushed back against me. I could feel her touching herself as my balls swung against her, I could scent the sex all around us, and I knew the mess her juices were making on her thighs. "Oh Jack, yes, please," she said, biting her lips and closing her eyes. I felt her hand flutter and then her ass grabbed me tight as she cried out aloud. She writhed against me, the ring of her tight asshole slipping up and down my cock, her *life* suffusing me in a deep, dark wave. I felt it slap against me, and I let it take me down.

"Angela," I groaned, pinning myself deep in her, still hard, until she finished with a moan. I let her catch her breath, and then she pouted, looking back, realizing I'd denied her.

"Why didn't you come for me?" she asked, sounding hurt.

I opened my mouth but knew I shouldn't tell her why—that I wasn't ready to give her up.

"Jack, it's not fair," she protested, pulling herself to all fours again.

I laughed. "I'm a vampire. Who the hell told you we were fair?" I stroked a hand down the curve of her ass to where it met the meat of her thigh, unwilling to meet her gaze.

She made a peeved sound and moved forward, set to pull herself off of me over this betrayal. I caught her waist before she could. "I don't want to stop fucking you," I confessed aloud. *Not tonight, and maybe not ever,* I kept to myself.

"Jack," she began, preparing to chastise me further, I thought, but she waited until I looked her in the eyes to continue. "It's not dawn yet," she said, her voice thick with promise, her lips pulling into a tempting smile as she wriggled back on me, grinding. "And you promised every which way."

I ground my teeth together. "*Fuck,*" I muttered, watching her, feeling her, making it a complaint, a verb, and an emotion. She laughed at that, which made her squeeze around me, and the sensation echoed up my spine and back down into my cock.

"And if this is my last night on earth, Jack," she went on, knowing full well she was going to get her way, "I want to slide into hell feeling broken."

I let go of her long enough for her to sway her ass temptingly, and then steadied her with a hand. "Broken, eh?" I asked, sliding both my hands up the gorgeous tattoos on her back. "No, Angela. I'd never break you," I told her. I reached beneath her to cup her breasts, and then suddenly pulled her back on me, her thighs spread wide across mine, her ass full of my cock. She gasped and threw her head back, and I both heard and felt her panting. I lightly wrapped a hand around her throat, so I could whisper darkly in her ear. "But if you want to go to hell, I know a devil you can dance with."

She trembled, in hope or fear I didn't know, and what was more, my hunger didn't care, I could feel my fangs piercing through my palate. We'd already tasted her twice, but it wasn't enough—it would never *be* enough—which was why I had to fight my urges.

"If you need me to stop, say so, okay?" I warned her.

She nodded frantically. "I'll try," she promised.

"I'll keep watch," I promised back, kissing below her ear, as I started to thrust.

I pushed and pulled her off of me, it was easy with my strength, making her ass pound against me, open wide. She ran one arm over her head, trying to clutch my back, while the other scrabbled for traction against my hip, trying to predict what was coming next, or control it, but I wouldn't let her. I grabbed her wrists to wind them together and hold them at her waist, using them to brace her as I thudded up. I reached between her legs with my free hand to bring her wetness up to grace her nipples and let the night air chill them, before sending my fingers back to stroke inside her.

"When I make you come again, Angie," I promised her, as I laced kisses down her neck, "I'm going to come too—and I'm going to bite you."

She made a low moan at that, but then said, "What if I don't?" and I caught a gleam in her eye as I looked up.

"Did I sound like I was giving you a choice?" I had her swollen clit beneath the pad of my middle finger, and every time I circled it I felt her hips tilt. I kissed a line across her shoulder, and then thrust up into her ass again. "If I keep doing this," I threatened, lifting her up and landing her on my cock, and shoving my fingers inside of her to rub her pussy's hot walls, before stroking her clit in a fast figure-eight, "do you think you'll be able to stop yourself?" I nuzzled my face into the space where her neck met her shoulder. "Do you think you'll *want* to stop yourself?" I whispered, knowing full well what the answer was.

Her breath caught in her throat and I could see her pulse pounding for me, same as I was pounding into her, not taking full strokes anymore, just one inch in, one inch out, forcing her ass to hold the hard thick length of me while I made the nerves of her tight asshole sing.

"Oh God, Jack," she said, making a groan of my name, and gave up any pretense of defiance, sagging back into my arms. Her breasts jiggled with every thrust, and she started moaning each time I filled her. "Jack—oh fuck," she whined. "*Jack.*"

"Yeah," I whispered in her ear. I held her pinned on me, my fingers shoved deep inside her, her pussy clenching them, begging them for release, but I didn't want to give it.

No, I wanted to keep fucking her like this forever—like if I fucked her hard enough, I could keep the dawn itself at bay. I ran my closed teeth up the side of her neck and felt her shudder. She wrenched a wrist free and grabbed hold of the back of my head, scratching nails against my scalp to keep me there.

"Please, Jack," she pleaded, willing to risk getting bitten if it meant she got to come, and suddenly it felt like I was not alone.

Like the devil I'd promised her was looking through my eyes experiencing every piece of her for the first time.

Her hot ass wrapped around my cock. My fingers in her soaking pussy—so wet her juices were dripping right down my sack and making a pool on the cement floor. The scent of sex in this small space was so overwhelming the night air couldn't blow it away. I could still taste her perfect cunt in my mouth and knew that her lips still tasted like my seed. She wriggled against me, shamelessly now, letting go of my hair to pull at her nipples, and I could see her blood soaring inside of her, almost like it was looking for a way out.

I had to help her.

She needed to come for me, so badly.

*And then I needed her to bleed.*

I let go of her other wrist and grabbed her hips, somehow getting harder, the thick head of my cock plunged so deep. "Fuck Jack, *fuck!*" she shouted, falling forward onto all fours, me following her forward, my balls high, my cock ramrod straight, mounting her with increased ferocity, fucking ready to give her my load. My fangs started sinking through the top of my palate, filling me with dire intent.

I pressed both of us to the ground, her face against her coat and clothes, covering all of her with my body, so she couldn't get away.

Her eyes squeezed shut and she whined, her hips trapped, pinned, whispering in her ear as I went still. "You're going to come, Angie, and you're going to come hard," I told her, and felt her shiver at the promise. "You know how I know?"

She shook her head beneath me, still trembling.

"Because I'm going to ask you to," I told her. I licked my lips and kissed her just below her ear. "Angela," I started, and I felt her brace herself, as I brought all of my vampiric powers to bear. *Come for me,* I demanded.

Her eyes flew open wide as she tensed and gasped. Her jaw dropped, and then she was fighting me with her wolf-strength—no, not fighting, just thrashing, coming, senselessly hard, her voice a silent scream. She bucked beneath me, her ass grabbing my cock like it was a gloved hand, begging for me to come with it.

Her orgasm washed out of her like a flash flood on the desert plain, dangerous, fast, and deep enough to drown in. I felt it push through me, through my flesh, and bone, and soul, and part of me hoped that it would be enough, while the rest of me knew it wouldn't be, it could never be, that nothing I ever did would ever make me stop.

I snarled as my fangs burst through and I planted them into her neck as I shoved her ass full of my cock.

She howled, crying out my name out in pain and satisfaction, and I knew my cum was spurting into her in hot waves at the same time as I was sucking her sweet blood out. My cock twitched hard against the walls of her ass, filling her up at the same time as I drank her down.

I closed my eyes, still fucking her. She tasted so exquisite, so perfect, so wonderful, like everything I ever had desired was rolled into each precious life-filled drop, and it was hard to imagine stopping. Why would I ever want to stop anything as marvelous and meant to be as this? I was still *fucking cumming*—no she was still making *me* cum—as I sucked her neck hard with each savage stroke.

*Oh God, I would never get enough of her, as long as I had her blood in me to keep me hard.*

We were at an edge I'd never reached before with Paco, or with anyone, and together we were so close to going over. Did she know it, could she tell? She moaned and shuddered in my arms like she was still coming—did she know how much it made me want to bite her until she couldn't anymore?

"Jack?" she whispered, her voice soft after so much shouting prior.

I snarled at her neck. I didn't want to hear her. Parts of me didn't want to know the truth, all the better to keep biting her—and the rest of me was scared of what I'd done.

"Jack," she tried again, more quietly.

I came to my senses in a rush, pulling back before my fangs were retracted, tearing her skin because it was safer than waiting. It broke the circuit and let me finish, deep inside her, with a final shudder and a grunt.

"Jack," she moaned. "Oh my God, Jack."

I swiped an arm against my mouth as I jerked back, pulling out of her entirely. "Are you okay?" I asked her, the second my fangs were short enough.

She turned to look back at me then, with some mixture of awe and reverence on her face. "Yeah." She reached up to touch her neck, found the blood on it with her fingers, and blinked back to reality.

I knew I'd misspoken earlier. I absolutely would break her if I let myself, and then that would in turn break me.

"I'm not safe and you shouldn't trust me," I told her, because it was the truth. If I fucked her again tonight, there'd be no going back, only carnage.

She closed her eyes and shook her head. "Shut up," she said, as she fell into my arms.

# CHAPTER TWENTY-TWO
## ANGELA

J ack wouldn't fuck me again after that, or even let me make him come again. He held me down, ate me out, stroked me, licked me—he wouldn't stop, pulling waves of pleasure out of me, even after I was sure I didn't have any more to give—but he'd scared himself, biting me, I could tell.

"Do I taste that good?" I asked him, cradled in his arms at the end of the night.

"You have no idea," he said, breathing rough. I looked up and caught him staring at the cement overhead. "It's going to be dawn soon, Angie."

I groaned. It wasn't fair—none of this was fucking fair. "No."

"I know," he said, sitting up. "But I've got to get back."

"I don't see any light."

"I feel it coming. And I need to shower. If I wake up smelling this much like you and you're not there...."

He didn't need to say anything else. I could see it in his eyes.

"All right," I admitted, and stood, picking up all the clothing I'd dropped.

In between carnalities, we'd planned this upcoming evening. I would go before moonrise and tell the Pack everything I knew. And then, when the full moon caught us all—we would see what'd happen. Rabbit was going with me—as was Jack, once again hidden in the back of the truck. I couldn't tell him what to do after he woke up, so I didn't try. I only hoped that if something bad happened to me or Rabbit, he would get away safely and tell Mark.

He stood as well, pulling on his jeans first, then tugging his silly green polo back on. The lean muscles of his back and arms rippled, and I had kissed each and every one of them. "If I had a camera, I'd take a picture of you in that to remember you by," I said.

"Don't say things like that. This isn't allowed to be final."

"Sorry," I said, and offered him my hand. He took it, and we walked quickly back to the hotel room together.

SHOWERS WERE AN ODDLY PRIVATE THING, considering everything we'd just put our bodies through—but maybe walls were good, maybe walls would stop us from hurting so bad later. I went first and came out to snuggle up against a still-sleeping Rabbit on my bed and when Jack came out, reclothed, he took to his own.

I was almost asleep, Jack had sexed all the adrenaline right out of me—but seeing Jack laying atop the bed over there, I knew he wouldn't be asleep until dawn.

"Hey," I whispered to him, over Rabbit's head. "C'mere."

He looked over at me, as though there were someone else in the room I could possibly be talking too, and then stood. I scooted back on the bed, and patted the space in between Rabbit and I. He hovered beside the bed, unsure.

"Let's pretend to be normal, Jack. Just for a minute."

I watched his chest lift and sink as he considered it, and then without saying a word he crawled up on the bed between us. Rabbit turned in his sleep toward him, throwing a careless arm over him as if he were me, and I folded myself up into his armpit on the other side, wrapping his arm around me. He nuzzled his face into my hair, I could feel the heat of his breath, as his thumb gently stroked my arm.

I would have said something, if I'd known what *to* say, but I didn't. *I'm sorry it had to be like this, but also thank you, and I'll never forget you, even if twelve hours from now I'm dead?* For his part, I knew he felt it too—and he kissed the top of my head.

I rubbed my head against his chest, and rested, listening for heartbeats, and could've sworn I heard some as I drifted off.

WHEN I WOKE UP, I woke up alone.

I startled up in bed. "Rabbit?"

"I'm peeing!" Rabbit announced from the bathroom.

I sank back. The clock on the nightstand said it was eleven a.m.. There was light creeping in around the edges of the blinds and—I leaned over the bed and looked underneath. Jack had built himself a cocoon under there, hiding from the world behind a wall of blackout fabric. I swallowed. Last night...everything we'd done to one another felt like it was all a dream. I remembered falling asleep against him and then him moving me to get back out of bed—

"Why's Jack asleep, Mom?" Rabbit asked, returning from the bathroom. I hadn't heard him wash his hands—I'd chide him for that later.

"Because he got worn out, honey."

"Rescuing me?" Rabbit asked.

"Something like that."

Rabbit and I spent the afternoon doing fun things. I went out and bought us ice cream, we colored, we played tag in the room, bouncing from bed to bed, laughing with glee. But once the clock rolled around to two p.m., I knew we had to go.

"Home?" Rabbit asked, watching me bend rebar I'd found alongside the road to replace the back window, wedging it into the truck's frame. "Oh, wait, grandma...." he said, remembering she was gone.

"No—not home. To meet other wolves. Tonight's a full moon night." The newspaper had said moonrise was at four-forty-five, sundown at five-fifteen. "We need to go talk to them."

"Why?"

"Because I need to tell them some things, and hope they believe me."

"I'll always believe you, Momma."

"Thanks, baby," I said, and smooched him.

Loading up the truck didn't take long—and I made sure to secure Jack in the back. He'd slide around a little again when we drove up to the new Farm, but he'd make it okay.

Along the way, Rabbit hit me with a litany of questions. "Where are the wolves?" "How many are there?" "How big are they?" "Are any of them little like me?" It was hard to stay patient with him and concentrate on the road—but maybe it was a good thing, because all his questions didn't leave any time for thinking.

I followed the path up that I'd taken down, and put the truck into park at four-thirty. I was cutting it close. I needed to be heard, but then I needed to change, because if I was a wolf, I didn't think Gray could cage me. I could already feel her, pushing against the surface of my skin, ready to come out.

The house in front of us was dark—so were the woods behind.

"You stay here," I told Rabbit, and hopped out of the cab.

They knew I was coming. And I knew that Gray was here—I closed the door quietly behind me—and saw a blur leap off the roof of the farmhouse, dropping onto the truck's hood, denting it into undrivability.

"Welcome back!" Daziel shouted. Rabbit screamed with surprise, and Daziel looked at him strangely. "You brought the boy?"

"Where's Gray? Where's Jonah?"

"Jonah's a fucking traitor, he is," Daziel said, jumping to the ground.

I swallowed. "From what I hear, you're the fucking traitor. You killed Wade."

"On my orders," Gray said, appearing in the farmhouse door. His body took up the entire frame of it. "I did it to prove my love to you—and it worked. Here you are, with David." He had the gall to be smiling at my son. Rabbit spotted him and ducked down beneath the dashboard.

"It didn't work, and you know it. I only came back here to finish things—and tell the truth." My voice rose and I hoped it carried. "Daziel and Murphy killed Wade on Gray's behalf! And they killed Bella, mate of Jonah, too!"

"Shut-up, girl," Daziel said, and punched me.

On any other night before this, it would've floored me. But now that I was silver-free, and with my wolf so close at hand—it dropped me for a second, and then I rebounded, jumping onto him, knocking him to the ground and bashing his head into the dirt. He threw me back and looked startled.

"Bella was pregnant! With a boy!" I shouted as loud as I could.

"So?" Gray said, advancing across the porch and coming down the stairs. "Who cares about her boy, when I have my own? Come here, David," Gray said, trying out his most fatherly tone on Rabbit.

"His name is Rabbit," I growled.

"No son of mine would ever tolerate being named that."

Rabbit peeked up over the edge of the dashboard—and hit the locks on both sides of the car. "Momma says you're a bad man!" he shouted.

"He is, baby. You'll see," I said low.

Daziel growled and raised his hand again—but Gray caught it. "That's your plan, isn't it."

I swallowed. I hadn't dared voice it aloud, but yeah, it was. I couldn't save Rabbit from the Pack—but if he watched Gray kill me —he would spend his entire life either planning to escape or plotting my revenge. Either way, he'd never belong to Gray. Not that I wanted to die though—or that I'd go down easy.

I leapt for Gray.

He caught me, as easily as someone swatting away a fly. He bashed me to the ground, and I heard Rabbit shout, "Noooooo!"

"You stay in there, baby!" I shouted back at him, kicking away from Gray on the ground. "So that's *your* plan? To just kill me in front of him? Or cage me? Like he won't smell my tears?"

"I wanted us to be a family—that's what I've always wanted, Angie. You know that about me. You remember you and me and Willa—"

"Who you murdered!" I screamed at him.

He went still and I could see the rage building inside of him. "It was an accident."

"And how many accidents have there been? Did the others not matter to you, too? Did you ever learn your lesson?"

The clock was ticking away, I knew we both could feel it, any minute now our wolves would arrive and make all of this moot—and whatever happened to us while we were wolves, our human selves would not remember. So if Gray just waited out the clock, he could always try to tell Rabbit he was wrong, that Daziel killed me, that maybe he tried to stop it but he was too late—so I played my final card.

"I'm the one who turned you in!" I shouted—at him, and for the benefit of anyone else listening. "So that no one else would die!"

Gray put his hands on his knees, looking half-way sick. "Too late."

# CHAPTER TWENTY-THREE
## JACK

I woke alone. In the bed of a truck, swathed in darkness—just like that time in the bodybag. I thrashed and got myself free, standing up—and found a sea of wolves watching a fight.

Buster squealed at seeing me—safe inside the truck's cab, where his mother had barred him in with rebar, his teeth too fat to pry up the doorlocks inside. I fell to a crouch, trying to figure out what was going on, while he tried to lick at me through the metal slats.

"Shh," I warned him—but none of the wolves, if they scented me, cared. All their eyes were on two wolves, wrestling. One of them was huge and gray, and I had a feeling I knew who it was. The other was also gray, but so light she was almost silver. I knew it was Angela—and I could both see and smell the way her coat was getting covered in her blood. Gray growled and leapt and she dodged and nipped at his underbelly, catching the spot where his hind-leg joined his torso—even as he twisted and firmly bit into her haunch. If it was a grinding game, he'd win, his jaw had to have twice her bite-pressure—without thinking, I leapt into the fray.

"Get the fuck off of her!" Whatever promises I'd made Angela were forgotten, as I pummeled at his face. His lips rose in a snarl, unwilling to let go of his bite. "She's not yours!" I said, kicking his stomach as hard as I could, feeling ribs break, knowing they were reknitting. "Let her go!"

Behind me, wolves growled, and I knew my freedom was about to come to an end when a huge black wolf appeared outside the circle, with shaggy hair in a leonine mane around him. He raced in, wolves parting to let him, and he barreled into Gray, taking him away from me and severing him from Angela, sending her and I sprawling. She whined, one leg limp, as I reached her side. There was a furless, scarred streak on her face, from the base of one ear down to her nose. I put a hand on her back, felt the springy give of her fur, she looked at me, and I knew—this was the creature I'd briefly seen the night prior. And she wasn't Angela. I'd call her Silver.

She whined at me, and then returned her attention to the new fight happening between Gray and Black. They growled and whirled, clawing and biting, each looking for a moment that would reveal the other's precious throat. Gray was injured—Silver hadn't managed to stay even, but she'd stayed alive, and in doing that, she'd gotten some bites in, and worn him down—and this new contender was fresh. They spun like duelists, waiting, and then—Gray snapped, attacking. Black feinted, and Gray made his mistake. He over-extended himself, trying to attack again, and misjudged Black's speed—because Black whirled and clamped his jaws down, on top of Gray's closed muzzle.

Gray made an alarming sound as Black's teeth ground in, scraping off the slender meat on either side of Gray's snout. Gray shook his head, but Black held him steady, his denser body absorbing each shudder as Gray fought to get free—and beside me, Silver came to attention. She ran in, and went for Gray's throat.

The sounds he made became dramatically worse, because they were coming out the holes she was making in him with her teeth. Then another wolf broke rank, a third, and a fourth—each of them choosing a different place on Gray to bite him. And just like that, the tide had turned. A wave of wolves rushed forward, all angling to get their piece of Gray, their dying leader, pulling mouthfuls of flesh from him, shredding him irreparably in the process. The scent of blood filled the air as intestines spilled out and stained the ground.

"Good God," I whispered, and looked back—Buster was watching from the truck cab with what I could only assume were wide-eyes, and I hoped to hell that Angela was right about their human selves not remembering.

And not long after that, Gray was gone. All that remained of him were disturbing chunks of fur and meat and bones too big to gnaw on and the remnants of a spine. Black released what remained of Gray's head, it hit the ground with a thump, and then he howled. A wolf broke rank, racing into the woods—and all of the others except Silver followed. I had a feeling I knew what they were going to do. Silver looked at me—and then looked past me, her almost-white eyes focusing on something behind.

I turned, and saw a slender black wolf crawling up, belly against the ground, carrying a piece of metal in her jaws. Silver growled, and this new wolf whined, twisting to offer Silver its neck and belly, letting the metal go. It was curved...a portion of a lock. And I could see where the teeth of the new wolf were broken and the fur around its jaws was stained with blood—had it gone and gnawed through metal?

Why?

I watched Silver inspect the scene, wondering what she was thinking, and then she placed her teeth on the new wolf's throat, delicately, almost like a kiss, before stepping back. The new wolf, now freed, rolled over, making sure to stay low to the ground as she crept away—and then Silver came up to me. I backed up until I was leaning against the truck, and heard Buster whining, scratching at the door. Her limp was healing—and I thought she was coming for my crotch, until I realized she was trying to get to Buster. I hopped into the back of the truck and reached through the cab to open up a lock with my ever-so-useful fingers, then leaped back down to pop the door. Buster jumped out and started snuffling Silver all over, and Silver looked up at me with eyes such a light blue they were almost white.

"Thanks for voting for me," I told her. She half-way closed her eyes and half-way rolled them, and then started licking Buster's face.

IF MOONRISE HAD BEEN before sunrise, it stood to figure that it would end before dawn too. I sat on the truck's cab, listening to the wolves hunt in the night, howling, and an hour or so before dawn, they returned as humans, staggering out of the forest naked and rough looking, a little like zombies. Their nudity was startling to me, but they didn't seem fazed—until they saw me, and started heading my direction.

"Hey," I started. "I'm a friend of Angela's."

A group of them conferred—and others looked over to where Gray's body had been left. The bones hadn't shifted back to human.

"Why're you still alive?" asked the man nearest me. He was as tall as I was and lean, with a beard that circled his chin, and shaggy black hair that covered his shoulders.

"Because he's not. Alive, that is." Angela answered for me, coming out of the forest. My breath caught. She was as disheveled as she'd been both above and below me the night before, and it was lovely to see all of her again. Rabbit was at her side, and shouted my name, before running over to scramble up the truck to join me.

"Let's find you some clothes, kiddo," I reached into the cab, and pulled out the tatters of his jeans.

"What do you mean by that?" the man asked Angela.

"He's a...." Angela began, and I heard her pause.

"Vampire," I jumped in, tying a shirt around Rabbit's waist like a kilt. "Fellow creature of the night. So maybe you didn't eat me out of professional courtesy."

The men—and women—looked to one another in disbelief.

"I know. I didn't think that you all existed until very recently, either. But you do and I do, hooray." I stood straighter and ruffled my hand through Rabbit's hair. "I saw everything last night—not that I know who did what, since all of y'all were furry—but I can try to explain what I saw happening. I have to hurry though—you all aren't the only ones on a clock."

The man now nearest me snorted. "All right. Try us."

PARSING out what had happened in the gap between them all becoming wolves but before the sun had gone down and I'd risen to witness things was a group effort. Gray had been sprung from prison and had locked Jonah up for freeing Angela on his return. But whatever small rebellion Jonah had started prior grew, as they realized Gray had ordered the death of someone named Wade. They wanted to know what happened to the three wolves who'd been sent to get Rabbit, who I'd buried underground, and they took the news of their deaths better than I would have—violence seemed to be a casual part of their lives. And then we came to discussing Bella.

"She was yours?" Jonah, who was now apparently their leader, asked.

"Bella? She didn't belong to anyone. That wasn't her style." I couldn't help but feel the weight of Angela's attention, standing nearby. I recognized another woman as well—Nikki, the one I'd met at Happyland's ball pit. She moved among their number, handing blankets out. "And it's not my style to claim people, either," I said, knowing Angela would hear me. "But she did say that she loved you."

"Was that before or after you slept with her?" His arms were crossed, and I could tell I was veering into dangerous territory.

"Actually, it was after she died. I spoke to her ghost." A murmur ran through the collected crowd, while he didn't move a muscle.

"Really?" he asked, his voice rich with disbelief.

"Yeah. I'm a vampire. Weird shit happens around me. Hazard of the occupation—but that's also when she gave me your name."

"And why would she have gone to you for protection, over me?" His voice was now like gravel, and I could sense his wolf lying just below his skin.

I eyed him steadily. "Guess that depends on what she needed protecting from—it wasn't vampires that killed her."

Jonah took a menacing step forward and Angela reached out a hand. "Someone knew she was pregnant, Jonah—and someone knew that if she had your child, you'd take the Pack. We couldn't see the pieces before, but now we can."

"Too bad everyone we could ask for answers is dead," said a man who'd introduced himself as Wyatt. I'd already noticed Daziel wasn't among their number anymore—I'd been looking at everyone's hands. I assumed his carcass was in the forest now, and what wasn't gnawed off had been left to rot.

"Not everyone," Nikki said. She hitched her blanket higher around herself, and the little girl from the ball pit stayed near to her. "She told me she was pregnant. Wanted to know what to do. I warned her." She cast glances around their group, daring anyone to challenge her. "I couldn't handle it anymore—I didn't want anyone else to die. Not like that."

Jonah jerked his chin at her, urging her to continue.

"Somehow, she already knew what she was getting into. She wanted the baby and the change, and she said she'd figure out a way to survive—and then she told me she'd succeeded."

The crowd went so quiet you could've heard a pin drop. It was then that I realized they were mostly men, and precious few women.

"I was ecstatic. I mean, if she figured out a way to keep women alive through their pregnancies, then—everything could change here. For the better. I told Daziel about it, and I thought he was as excited as I was—but then Bella's mood changed and she left. When I'd heard she'd died I'd assumed things hadn't worked out. Because they almost never do."

"When instead what'd happened is Daziel and Murphy went to murder her," Angela said. "Because that kind of power would've been a threat to Gray."

Nikki nodded. "Because they didn't care about what happens to us," Nikki said, sharing a look with Angela.

Jonah rounded on Nikki almost faster than I could see. "You got her killed!" He grabbed her by the neck and hoisted Nikki high. Her blanket fell to the ground as her daughter shrieked.

"Jonah, no!" Angela shouted, reaching for her.

"Her, and my child!" Jonah's arm started to shake in anger, as his other arm swatted Angela back. "Aren't you mad at her too? Didn't she lure you and your friend in?"

Angela stopped at that. "She did. But that was a long time ago, Jonah. And she was only a small part of a much bigger problem—"

"Well there's no one else here to kill now for it," he growled darkly.

Nikki's daughter squealed. Her hair was black, just like her mother's—and I remembered the crawling black wolf that I'd seen earlier that night.

"Put her down!" I shouted, just on the verge of whammying him. Jonah looked over his shoulder to glare. "How'd you get out of the cage? Because I was the only one here with thumbs last night, and it wasn't me!" I ran past him, out into the field where Gray had died. "A black wolf brought this up—one with broken teeth and a bleeding jaw." I found the piece of metal and tossed it at Jonah's feet.

He slowly set Nikki down, shoving her away, before picking the metal up—it looked like the curve of a lock to me.

He sniffed it, eyeing her. "Your wolf did that?"

Nikki held her throat. "I don't know," she said hoarsely. "All I know is that I wanted her to—right before I changed."

Jonah looked at her intensely, and she seemed to wither underneath his gaze. "You are forgiven," he said, and then drew her near. He licked a streak across her forehead as though giving her his blessing, and then he turned to face the group. "No Pack member is ever going inside a cage again." He hurled the piece of metal into the forest, then spoke again to the throng. "I'm pack leader now. Your wolves know the truth—but do you agree?" Whoops filled the air, along with howls from human throats. Even Rabbit cheered, excited to have something to cheer for. I gave Angela a helpless look, and she smiled back at me—and then I felt dawn hitting, hard. I closed my eyes and tilted my head—the international sign for 'it's almost bedtime'—so she came and took my hand.

I let her lead me into the farmhouse. There was still a ruckus going on outside, but the wolves had all day to celebrate, so why not? I had no doubt that soon they'd all be drinking, hollering, and eating breakfast—while I'd be dead in a closet somewhere.

Angela led me upstairs, and into a small room. "I think this is safe. It smells like Nikki, and she owes you, big time." She opened up a door and pulled on a light.

"Closet. Called it."

"Sorry," she said, giving me a sad smile. She let me go in first, pushing my way past all sorts of clothing, making a space among shoes on the floor. The way she stood—the tension in her shoulders —I knew, but I still needed to hear her say it.

"You're not going to be here when I wake up, are you?"

She licked her lips. "Sorry, Jack." She stepped in after me, closing the door behind herself with a sigh. "If we stay here too long, Rabbit will get ideas."

I nodded. But just because I knew it was coming didn't mean it didn't hurt. "You still want to raise him human?"

"Yes. But without silver. I'll figure something out." She glanced back, as though she could see through the walls, into her past. "The Pack doesn't make its money investing in stocks, Jack. This isn't the life I want for him."

And neither was mine, my unlife, that is. No matter what I felt about her, or toward her—or Rabbit, for that matter—it didn't change who I was. I swallowed and braced, trying to steel myself against her loss. "You think Jonah's honorable?"

She blinked, considering this. "Yeah. He won't come after me."

I wasn't going to ask her how she could be so sure. "Back at Bella's—her spirit showed me some things. I thought they were recipes, like for food, but it seems more likely they're for magic. She was a smart girl, if she came up with a cure for their pregnancy curse, she'd write it down." I watched Angela's jaw drop as I spoke. "The books are behind her water heater."

She rocked back on her heels. "I'll tell them. Maybe the Pack could afford to hire one of those magicians to help, too, now that their priorities are realigned. If they could look at her notes...."

"She was always saying she could cast spells. I just didn't believe her in time."

Angela nodded quickly. "It's a chance worth taking. Even though Rabbit and I are leaving, these are my people—and Jonah's not the type to do science for science's sake."

I nodded too, trying to stop from fading away, fighting dying for as long as I could. "I can't believe I'm not going to see you again, Angela."

"You might," she said with a soft sad smile. "You just shouldn't count on it for the next decade or so. And—it's never going to be like this," she said, gesturing between us. I couldn't help myself, I caught her hand. She didn't fight, so I pulled, and she was in my arms and my face was in her hair, her body pressed against mine. "I have to go back, Jack," she whispered, and I knew what she meant—to her normal boyfriend and her somewhat normal occupation and to being a normal mom.

"I know. I do too." Somewhere back in Vegas, Paco was probably worried sick about me—and I would still need to feed most every night. There was never a world in which *we* happened or worked. We'd been lucky to get the time we did. I felt compelled to say something, I wasn't sure what, but she tilted her head up to kiss my jaw and my lips found hers. I'd never fought dawn for so long before, trying to drink her in.

"Don't fight it," she said when she pulled back, in imitation of me before I'd bit her in the hotel bathroom. I sank, pulling her with me to the closet's floor. "Don't fight it, Jack. I love you. Don't fight," were the last sounds I heard.

# CHAPTER TWENTY-FOUR
## JACK

I woke up in a closet, alone. I sat up—and something metal rattled off my chest. I caught it and stood, turning the light on.

It was Angela's keyring for Dark Ink Tattoo. The front door, the office door, and the cabinet where she hid the good coffee. It was all mine, now that she was leaving.

"Thank you," I whispered, still feeling bereft. How could I explain to anyone what'd happened? I couldn't tell them the truth, obviously —I'd have to come up with a really good lie. Who knew how many artists had already quit or clients moved on, pissed that the place was closed? Its rep would be in the toilet—but a 'new ownership' sign could change all that. I opened the closet door and stepped out into the bedroom—and found Nikki, perched on the bed, wearing yoga pants and a t-shirt.

"Hey," I said, pocketing the keys.

"I couldn't really go to sleep until you were gone."

"Understandable. Sorry to keep you waiting. Your closet's nice, thanks."

She snickered. "There's a truck outside—one that'll run. We left you the keys. We'll need it back, but not for a few days."

"Thanks. I was wondering how I was going to get out of here—I was a little worried someone was going to make me ride a motorcycle."

"Nah," she said, with a grin. "Not in that outfit."

I looked down at myself. "Yeah. Usually I'm much more fashionable—or at least vampire appropriate."

She shook her head. "I can't believe I hit on you at Happyland. You could've killed me."

I raised my hands, protesting innocence. "That's really not my style. And besides, you were under orders."

"I was, but, some of that was me." She tossed a wave of black hair back. "I mean—my wolf—she like *really* likes you."

I chuckled. "It's not your fault—I have it on good authority that vampires are werewolf catnip."

"You and Angela?" she asked, raising her eyebrows.

"Yeah." Memories of my last moments with her came flooding back. She'd said she'd loved me, and I believed her. "Is she okay?" I asked softly.

"Yeah. Jonah gave her a ride into town. We had her phone and keys from that night—she and her boy are on their way elsewhere."

"They didn't say where?"

"No. Sorry."

I swallowed and nodded. "It's for the best." I'd known Angela was really gone the second I'd found Dark Ink's keys on my chest.

"Yeah. She thought so. We talked. And," she tilted her head, making her black hair spill across her shoulders, "she told me some things." She stood up and crossed the room toward me.

"Like what?" I asked, before remembering this morning. I'd just been outed as a vampire to an entire gang of werewolves. "Oh —*fuck*," I said, as realization sank in.

"Yeah, that, pretty much," Nikki said, giving me a look and running the tip of her tongue across her upper lip. "I don't want to get bitten," she went on, pulling off her shirt. "But Angela promised me that you'd fuck me like your life depended on it."

I inhaled slowly. She was beautiful, her body was tight, and I could smell that she was willing. I hadn't eaten at all yesterday, and while the feast Angela'd given me the night before had kept me sated, it wouldn't last forever—nothing could.

"I...." I began, staring at her, feeling the hunger wake. "I can't. Not right now. I haven't been home in days."

"Oh, come on," she protested. "What's a few more hours? Or even a few more minutes?"

"I need to get back, and check on things. I'm sorry."

She groaned and pulled her shirt back on. As I took a step toward the door I could almost feel my hunger rotate to keep an eye on her, like a separate thing.

*It was what I was and who I was, no matter how much I didn't want it to be.*

I stopped with my hand on the doorknob. I'd be able to keep the memory of Angela sacred for one night, but no more.

"Nikki," I said, so I'd know I had her full attention, as I let my voice drop low and looked back. "When we do fuck, because we will —I promise you it'll be so good I'll make you beg me to do things to you that you're not proud of later."

Her eyes widened, then squinted. "That's what men always think."

I gave her a knowing look, half-myself, half-my-hunger. "Yes, but I'm a vampire. Give me your phone."

She handed it over, I programmed my number in, and called myself so I'd have her number, and then I handed it back. "I'll ring."

"We'll see if I answer," she said, taking it from me.

I looked down at her, eyes full of intent. "You will," I promised her.

After that, I was down the stairs and out the door.

# JACK

THE TRUCK they'd left for me looked bad, but ran well—I drove down south, out of the hills and back into Vegas. I couldn't wait to get back to my place, take a shower, and get yelled at by Sugar for being gone so long and coming home smelling like dogs.

Then, I would put on clothing that I liked that fit me, and I would sit back on my couch and watch TV. Do a few drawings. Make a plan for Dark Ink. Figure out how to pay back Zach for cat-sitting in interesting ways. Call Paco, and let him yell at me too, and then figure out when I could go over to his place again. Maybe even let him come over to mine, at long last—

I was still daydreaming about all the possibilities when I pulled into my apartment complex and parked. I'd have to figure out which tow lot my Betty had most likely been taken to tomorrow night. Maybe I'd get extremely lucky, and she'd still be at Mark's.

I walked up to my door with a spring in my step, found the key underneath the mat where Zach had left it—good man—and unlocked it to walk in. Everything was dark, and sure enough, Sugar started to yowl.

"I know, I hear you—I know," I said, shutting the door behind myself, and flicking on some lights. My phone was still on the charger on the bar. I picked it up out of habit, and saw that I had twenty missed calls or so, a hundred texts—*Jesus, Paco*, I thought and smiled, without opening any of them up.

I was sure he was pissed about how I'd shooed him off, and that he'd been non-stop worried about me ever since—but I was glad of it.

Glad that someone in my life was still around to care, and that somehow he and I were able to make this work, exactly as it was. Paco might want more from me, and might be angry at my vampire-side for stopping us from having that, but he wasn't going to pull away.

I meant everything I'd said to him that night at Mark's before I'd blown him—I would be a part of his life for as long as he would have me.

And that, I realized, was probably the only thing stopping me from falling apart now. Not that he and Angela were interchangeable —because they weren't, my thoughts and feelings about both of them occupied very different parts of my soul.

But just knowing that he was there for me now and that he always would be—Paco's presence in my life was like a lighthouse, shining enough light into my dark to keep me safe.

A knock at my door disturbed me from my thoughts. Zach? Stalking me, until I got back? That was a little intense, but he was young—I swiped a hand over my face, and walked back for it, wondering if he'd ever sleep with me again if he saw me in these shoes.

"Hello?" I said, swinging it open.

A tall woman dressed in black and wearing a velvet choker stood there, holding a phone up—and on the phone was what appeared to be a live video of Paco, bound and gagged. My heart fell into my stomach.

"The clock has begun. If you're not at Vermillion within the next ten minutes, my Mistress will begin wringing your lover's neck."

Vermillion was fifteen minutes away on a good day. "Shit, fuck, fuck, FUCK!" I shouted, increasingly loudly, as I grabbed my keys and ran for the door.

# CHAPTER TWENTY-FIVE
## JACK

I *should've*—I thought, hauling the junky truck around corners like it could bend. I should've kept him safer, somehow. I should've never been with him. I should've never fallen for him.

And I should've grabbed that girl and dragged her with me to interrogate along the way. She'd fallen back, and I'd ran past her out the door without thinking. But she'd been mortal, clearly—there'd been panic in her eyes when she'd backed up.

Goddammit all to hell—I dragged the wolves' unfamiliar truck over curbs and ran reds, until I threw it into park and heard the transmission crunch in Vermillion's parking lot. I ran inside without thinking and found a full house.

*"Anyone who doesn't want to die tonight LEAVE NOW!"* I bellowed over the music. Everyone inside paused—and then people started rushing out in a panicked wave, men, women, dancers. The hostess left her station, the bartender jumped over the bar, men raced past with their flys down and their dicks still out, girls tottering out topless into the night—until I was looking at a much smaller number of people.

It was a strip club on a weekday. Of course some of the people in here wanted to die.

*"Everyone who's human—OUT!"*

That rattled the rest of them free as I stalked toward the back. I knew where I would find her—and him.

"Jack. Finally!" Rosalie announced. Paco was tied to a chair and the chair to the pole on center stage—the same place I'd found Thea dancing, all those years ago.

"Let him go," I growled.

She ignored me. "Do you think I don't know what you did?" Paco was bruised, he'd been beaten—but at seeing me, he started shaking his head, warning me to stay away.

If he thought I could, he was a fool.

"I didn't do anything, Mistress. Your man broke your deal and sold my charge out to werewolves. All I did was fight back. Some helpful human had gone and left bombs." I made my voice calm and walked up to the podium, trying to hide my shaking. "The place exploded—but the boy survived. Your deal is intact."

"*My deal*," she snarled, derisively.

"Isn't that all there is in life? Survival? Money?"

"You and I both know that that is not the case." She traced a hand down Paco's face, as if testing the quality of his shave. "Don't make me make you tell me."

If I told her I'd killed Tamo, there was nothing to stop her from taking Paco's life. I steeled myself to not give anything away.

"I keep telling you what I'm afraid of, Jack," she went on. "Cameras. Technology. That doesn't mean that I can't use them, though. I saw you. I watched you plunge a finger into his eye and stir his brains." One of her hands crept, so that she could tap a fingertip on Paco's eye that was swollen shut. Her finger pressed in and he winced.

"You're right—I killed Tamo!" I shouted, and ran three steps closer. "So kill me! Not him!"

"Silly man. Why wouldn't I just kill the both of you?" Rosalie laughed. "The only decision I have to make now is how will it hurt you more? To watch him die, knowing you couldn't save him—or for you to die, knowing that your lover's doomed?" She lounged over Paco. "If I could get you both to die at the exact same time, I would. Maya!" She shouted Maya's name, and Maya emerged from the back. She was wearing her dancing clothes and heels, and looked as unprepared as I was.

"Maya, kill your brother here, would you?" Rosalie said, tilting her head in my direction.

"But...." she began.

"*Kill Jack,*" Rosalie growled, and Maya propelled herself forward. Her body and her expression were at odds—she knew how to kill, she'd clearly done it before—but her face said she didn't want too.

"What's happening?" she asked, of Rosalie, and of herself, as Rosalie's command overwhelmed her.

"Don't listen to her, Maya," I said, falling into a crouch. "I don't want to hurt you."

"Too bad," Rosalie tsked. "Because I'm going to start strangling your man now. And you've got to get through Maya, to get to me." Rosalie wrapping a hand around Paco's throat.

"NO!" I screamed and bolted for the stage—and Maya caught me, with an arm across my gut, sending me swinging to the side and down.

"Aww, *fuck*, Jack!" Maya yelled, as if it were my fault she was about to stomp on my face with her heels.

"I don't want to hurt you, Maya!" I shouted, grabbing her leg and twisting her down. She fell on to her hands, and I still had her by the ankle.

"Then don't!" she shouted back at me.

I kicked her in her stomach, sending her skidding across the floor, knocking down chairs like bowling pins. I could've broken her leg, or ripped it off of her—but actually killing her would've taken time and I didn't want to—I just needed to get to Paco's side. I could see him going limp, and watch his blood start to stutter as lack of oxygen panicked his heart. I raced for the stage and stepped onto it.

"*Not one step further,*" Rosalie said—and my body obeyed. "How's it feel, Jack?" I could hear Maya behind me, standing back up, running toward me in heels. "To know that I've taken everything you ever loved in this world from you?"

Before I could respond, Maya's arm looped around my neck and dragged me back. I went with her and we fell in a wrestling tumble.

"I hate her," Maya whispered in my ear.

"Then fucking fight," I whispered as she choked me. Paco was dying and there was nothing I could do.

"I am! That's why you're still alive!" she said, through gritted teeth.

"*Then fucking fight her,*" I growled at Maya.

"Don't you fucking start with me too!" she shouted back. But her arms loosened, and I slipped through.

"It doesn't matter," Rosalie said, as I stood back up. "It's done."

I stood there, swaying. She was right. Paco's heart had stopped. His blood was drifting down through him on its final course, like the last raindrops of a summer storm, evaporating on a hot night before they landed.

The man that'd saved me from myself, who taught me how to make some peace with what I was, who had given me some semblance of hope that I had clung to each morning when I died, was gone.

And that Jack—the one that Paco had loved—died with him.

I felt all my humanity disappear, leaving only a vast darkness behind. "Get away from him!" I snarled at her, expecting to be obeyed.

I didn't recognize my own voice, and it didn't matter. I felt the eternity of all my future days without Paco in them weighing on me now, compressing my hatred for Rosalie like the hammer of a gun.

She was going to die tonight or I was.

"You don't order me!" she snapped.

"*GET AWAY FROM HIM!*" the dark thing that I'd become roared.

Rosalie staggered back under the weight of my command, as I leaped up to Paco's side, wracked with grief, things breaking in me that time would never repair. "What've you done?" I said, half to her, half to myself. "What have you done?!"

"Nothing that time wasn't doing already!" Rosalie shouted back in self-defense. Her eyes were wild and I could taste her fear pricking in the room. Emotions, foolish human emotions, came rushing back to me, and I sank to my knees, sagging against Paco. I placed my head in his lap and wrapped my arms around his legs. He was still warm, for now, warmer than I was.

"I'll punish you later," I heard Rosalie tell Maya. "And I'll punish you, now," she promised me, coming back. "What did you ever see in him, Jack, that was worth losing your life over?" she asked, stroking Paco's hair off his face.

I found her answer, and mine, clipped on the inside of Paco's left boot. I shifted, and quietly pulled out what I knew would be a silver knife as I answered her.

"I loved him because he loved me, even though he knew the score," I said, lunging up, blade out, plunging it into her side.

The silver ripped through Rosalie's dress and the skin behind it parted like it'd been sewn on the same seam, her organs spilling out like piñata candy. Rosalie was aghast for a moment, and then she screamed—a sound not meant to be heard by human ears—and started sifting through the slick wet tubes that'd fallen, trying to shove them all back in. Maya ran up beside me, one heel in her hand.

"I hate you! I fucking hate you!" she said, stabbing the heel of it into Rosalie's back.

"I made you, Jack!" Rosalie hissed, her fangs halfway out, unable to comprehend my betrayal.

"I didn't ask to be made!" I shouted back—as the pieces of her around my ankles started to shift to sandy dust, then all of her collapsed, leaving a torn dress and a foul smell.

"Oh my God. Did we do it?" Maya said, still holding her heel in one hand. She kicked off her other heel, and then looked at me. I was still holding silver—were we still fighting? I didn't care anymore. I dropped the knife, and turned back toward Paco, unable to come to grips with the enormity of what I'd lost. He'd been the only one who'd always understood me.

*My lover, my friend, my mate.*

Maya reached out and put a hand on my arm. "If you want him, try."

It took me a second to realize what she was suggesting. "He's dead."

"So are you."

Would he want to live...like this? Like me? Could I condemn him to that? Could I live my life without him?

Not if there were a way to change that.

I bit my wrist, hard, tearing a chunk out so that it wouldn't heal right away, and then put it to his lips, opening his jaw. "Come on. *Come on*," I said, kneeling over him, squeezing my forearm to make it bleed faster. I knew my blood was rolling down his throat into his stomach, but was there any of his life left for it to quench and replace with the un-life that I knew? I pressed my head to his and whispered in his ear, "Don't die on me. I can't make it without you."

I stayed pressed against him as the room spun, waiting for a sign, as Maya rose up, ripped his shirt open, and touched him.

"You're not going to feel a heartbeat," I said like she was stupid. I didn't want her touching him—I only wanted people who loved him to touch him from here on out. I pulled my wrist from his mouth. The wound was healed, but I would never be. I took his head between my hands, set my forehead to his, and felt sorrow wrack me. He was gone because of me, just like I'd always feared would happen.

My lighthouse was gone, and I was shattered on the shore.

"Jack," Maya said, shoving at his chest.

"*DON'T TOUCH HIM,*" I snarled at her, and she yanked her hand back like it was on fire. I grabbed the knife and cut through the ties that held him to the chair to pull him toward me, his slack body sagging into my arms, as I helplessly wept. I moved to pick him up, cradling him to me. I didn't know where I would take him, I only knew he deserved better than this.

*And he deserved to have been loved by someone better than me.*

"*Jack,*" Maya said, with emphasis but without a whammy, and set her hand against my cheek. It was cold, like it'd just been in a freezer. "Jack, he's dead—but in a good way."

I inhaled, finally hearing her, and feeling him. Everywhere we touched I could feel the chill of the grave permeating from his body.

Maya was right—Paco was dead...just like I was.

"You saved him," Maya said, growing bold, an unfamiliar smile on her face. "Because of my good advice. So—you owe me. The clubs are mine. Both of them."

"Yeah, sure, whatever." I dropped the knife and held him closer.

I just wanted to get us home.

# CHAPTER TWENTY-SIX
## JACK

I carried Paco across the threshold into my apartment, set him into the coffin on my bed, and kissed his bloodstained lips.

We'd never talked about me changing him before, because it seemed impossible. I never would've put him in danger—in *more* danger—with Rosalie.

So I didn't know exactly how he'd wake up. I could only hope that he'd be happy that he was still with me.

I showered, fed Sugar, and sat down on my couch, letting mindless TV wash over me, trying not to think.

And then around three there was a gentle knock outside my door. I answered it and found Zach outside in his uniform. "The key was missing," he said, looking hopeful. "I figured you came home."

"I did indeed." I raked a hand through my loose hair. "Thanks for cat sitting. I appreciate it."

Zach's warm smile cranked a few sunbeams brighter. "You're welcome. Did you have fun? Wherever it was that you were?"

"It was a long few days," I said, honestly.

"Well...I've got half-an-hour," he said, still grinning.

I knew what he was hinting at, shook my head, and closed my eyes. "Sorry, Zach. Not tonight."

His full lips fell into a small pout, but then he shook his shoulder once, like he was twitching off a fly. "Sure. You're probably tired and all."

"Actually, I am." I went to grab the door behind him. "I'll see you around though, all right?"

"Yeah," he said, stepping back with a sigh.

I moved to close the door, but made the mistake of looking out after him as he walked down the hall in the ill-lit dark.

One of the lights our landlord needed to replace stuttered, making Zach cast crazy shadows on the wall, like there was a monster chasing him.

*Was there?* I wondered, as I licked a line across my upper teeth.

I wanted him, because I was a creature of want. Of need. Of hunger and desires.

But...I'd come back from whatever I'd been when I'd been buried in Angela, cock and fang. I hadn't taken too much, and I hadn't gone over.

And I'd come back from whatever I'd been when I thought Paco had died—my murderous rage had ended the second I'd brought Paco 'back.'

Which meant it was still *me* standing here.

And what was more, with Rosalie gone...I was finally free.

I knew the darkness that Bella had warned me about would always be a part of me...but for right now, for the space of tonight, I'd survived it.

That seemed worth celebrating.

*It was worth a hand-job, at the very least.*

I grinned and put my fingers to my lips to whistle loudly. Zach's head whipped back, looking over his shoulder. "Get your ass back here," I growled low, so it would echo toward him.

"Yeah?" he asked, his voice going high with hope.

"Don't make me ask twice," I teased, stepping back from the

door. He raced to follow me inside. "You got any sick time?" I asked as I closed the door behind him. He nodded quickly. "Use it, if you don't mind," I said, before answering the unspoken question in his eyes. "Because I'm going to need you for longer than thirty minutes."

His eyebrows went up and he fished his phone out, instantly feigning getting sick to a manager. I went for my phone as well and waited for him to finish. "Do you mind women?"

"Uh—generally, no? But I don't really know what to do with one, if that's what you're asking. They're not my thing."

"Do you object to one's presence?" I asked. I knew the last number that'd called me had to be Nikki's.

"No."

"Good." I texted Nikki my address, then gave Zach the kind of look that made his blood flow south—I knew because I could see it.

Mine was, too, just thinking about the things I would do to the both of them.

"Why do you ask?" he asked, the very voice of intentional innocence. I leaned in and pressed him against the door, kissing him hard until I felt his hips try to thrust, his body begging me for more. I pulled my head back, leaving him aching, I knew.

"Because," I said, rocking into him with promise, so that he knew exactly what he was getting into. "After the night I've had—I need to get a lot of people off."

I gave him a dangerous smile and went for the buttons at his throat.

FIND OUT WHAT HAPPENS WHEN PACO WAKES UP IN
BLOOD AT DAWN: DARK INK TATTOO BOOK FIVE
READ ON FOR A SNEAK PEEK.

# BLOOD AT DAWN
## DARK INK TATTOO BOOK FIVE
### JACK

I woke up in my coffin with Paco's hair tickling my cheek.

Waking up in the same coffin as my currently dead best friend and lover was awkward—and it would only get worse when in three days he woke up too. I hadn't gotten a chance to ask his permission before turning him into a vampire. It'd been that or watch him die, and I'd acted without thinking. I knew he'd wake up hungry—I could only hope he wouldn't wake up mad.

I kissed the back of his neck and rose up, to Sugar's meowing. "I know, I know, I hear you." I swung one leg over the partition that kept the sleeping dead like me safe from tiny carnivores like her. She wound through my legs on my way to the kitchen. "I know," I repeated, pouring out a bowl of food. "It must be scary when I die every morning, huh? You must wish you had opposable thumbs." She purred while she ate, a sound that was charming even if it wasn't melodious. I was leaning down to scratch her behind her ears when the door rang.

I tensed. Who was left in town that knew where I lived? I'd already made plans via text with the Dark Ink Tattoo crew to meet tonight. Angela and Mark were gone by now, Paco was in my bedroom already, and Zach and Nikki I'd both slept with last night. Nikki had left a bra behind as an excuse to come back, but I was sure she had pride, she would bide her time before calling for it. Zach, however, lived in my apartment complex—and had gotten used to getting lucky. He was also the only one of my recent lovers who didn't know I was a vampire—I needed to cut him loose for his own safety. The doorbell rang again, followed by an impatient knock.

"Look," I said, swinging the door open, ready to say something drastic. But it wasn't Zach, it was a woman, the same one who'd brought me the news of Paco's torture last night. "You," I said, letting my voice fall.

"Me," she said, giving me a nervous smile. "I'm Luna. And you're—"

"Angry," I cut her off.

She fidgeted, clearly nervous. "May I come in?"

"No." I stepped back into my apartment and closed the door.

I SHOWERED and pulled on the most business appropriate clothing I had, a white t-shirt, a blue button down with a crisp collar, jeans that were a solid deep blue, and black cowboy boots. Paco would've been proud of me if he were currently alive, he was by far the more dapper of the two of us. I slicked my hair back and tried my best to give the bathroom mirror a business face. It was hard. I was used to doing whatever the hell I wanted to, which included not taking work very seriously.

But that was changing tonight. Before Angela had left she'd given me Dark Ink Tattoo—Las Vegas's only 24/7 tattoo parlor. It was the perfect cover for a vampire who could feed on sex or blood: I loved doing tattoos, I got to work nights, and the clientele was often interested in seeing the non-tattoo side of me after dark. Being the giving sort, I did my best to never leave anyone disappointed. But if I wanted to keep it going I needed to step up—which meant facing eight to twelve probably pissed off tattoo artists shortly.

They'd been out of work ever since Angela had closed up shop a few days ago to deal with her werewolf problems. I'd helped her survive and we'd consummated years of mutual lust in one glorious night. But she was gone now, leaving me with an emptiness that was different from my normal hunger. I didn't have many long-term people in my life—being a vampire was, in general, too dangerous. And while being with Angela had been magnificent—and I would never forget the taste of her skin, her cunt, her blood—I knew I'd only just started missing her. She'd been a rare constant presence in my life, such as it was. Someone who trusted me, and in whom I could trust.

*An actual friend.*

I couldn't begrudge her her new life though. She had a son—and a far more appropriate human boyfriend, Mark. They were probably halfway across the globe now, which was where they belonged, having a normal life.

I, on the other hand, was abnormal—and I'd made Paco match me.

I fought the urge to return to my bedroom and look at him again. I loved him too, in my own way—I always had, ever since he'd first come onto me in that crowded club, after our first desperate fuck. He'd been my first time with another man. And if he left me after this like Angela had—I couldn't bear to think about it now, my eternity stretching on alone, with no one who truly knew me at my side. The thought of it was too frightening—and I needed to go back to Dark Ink now and try acting like a boss.

I grabbed my wallet and the keys to a truck loaned to me from the werewolf pack, made sure the lid was closed on the coffin for Paco's safety, then emerged out my front door—to find that same girl still waiting.

"Hi!" she said, her face brightening. "I'm pledged to you. As a bloodslave."

I looked around to make sure no one else in the complex could hear. "I don't need you," I harshly whispered. "And I don't want you."

Her face crumpled. She was very gothy, long black hair with straight bangs and oval ice-blue eyes, like a cat's. She'd been in some sort of dress last night, but today she was in black leggings, clunky boots, and a low-cut black t-shirt so tight I could tell she wasn't wearing a bra. A small backpack was slung over her shoulders. "I only have a few hours left."

I pulled my door shut behind me and locked it, ignoring her.

"I just need you to say yes," she went on, following me out to my truck, making me regret the distance to it in the parking lot. "Please. I have to serve someone. I can't be unowned."

I unlocked the door to the truck and sat inside, closing it resolutely on her.

"What're you going to do when he wakes up, huh?" she shouted at my window. How did she know about Paco? Had Maya told her?

She ran around to stand in front of the truck. "Don't make me go back to Maya—please."

"Get the hell out of the way," I said, knowing that even with my windows up she could see my lips and read the look on my face.

"You're going to have to drive over me!" She put both hands on the hood, flashing her cleavage as her chest heaved with intent. "I'm dead if I go back to her." I revved the engine and she started to shout over it. "Bloodslaves can only be free for twenty-four hours! I've only got five hours left to find a new Master to claim me, and we both know if you were going to kill me you would've done it already!"

I wrung the steering wheel. At least it was dark out. An unknown to me neighbor walked by, neck craning back at our scene. I tried to keep a low profile on principle, and hoped that anyone else seeing this would write it off as LARPing or kinky roleplay. And I hoped to hell Zach wasn't looking out of his window, I didn't need anything else to explain to him.

"Come on!" she shouted at full volume, shoving the car hard

enough to make it shake. I leaned over and unlocked the passenger door.

"Get in."

"Thank you, thank you, thank you," she said, settling herself beside me, swinging her backpack beneath the dashboard.

"Who's to say I'm not taking you out to the desert to snack on?"

"Rosalie promised me you weren't like that, last night." When Rosalie had sent her over here to tell me Paco was in danger. Maya and I had murdered our Mistress, and now we were free.

"Yeah, well, Rosalie's dead," I said, gruffly. The girl looked down and put her hands between her knees. "Sorry?" I guessed. I wasn't, really, but I didn't know what else to say.

"I know why you had to do it. Not that that makes it okay."

"She started things, if it makes you feel better," I said. "Where should I take you?"

"What?" She sounded genuinely surprised.

"I'm not in the market for a bloodslave."

"But—you should be. You need one. All vampires do."

"I've been fine so far." I shrugged a shoulder. I'd only found out about the existence of bloodslaves recently—when I'd run from Rosalie after my making, I'd had to find my own paths to blood and sex. Luckily, I lived in Las Vegas. If I played my cards right, I could practically get both delivered.

"But!" she sputtered.

"Yeah, so—here?" I ignored her. "Downtown?" I gestured at the strip malls we passed by.

She turned to face me fully, eyes expressive. "But if you don't claim me, then Maya will." Her eyeliner was perfect, winged out wide. "Would you want to serve Maya?"

"Not particularly. But I also don't want to own a slave. Apart from the ethical considerations, it seems like a lot of responsibility."

She wriggled in her chair. Certain parts of me suddenly woke to watch her—just as other parts of me were annoyed at them for waking. I'd feasted last night on sex with Zach and Nikki both—why couldn't my hunger just leave me be? "Maybe—you could just pretend you own me?" she asked.

I'd been driving to Dark Ink Tattoo out of habit. I couldn't drive past it—I needed to get myself together, to pull my Jack Stone tattoo-artist-extraordinaire and vampire-businessman persona on. "I don't owe you anything."

"I know. But—you wouldn't want to know what Maya would do to me—she hates me."

"That's not my problem," I growled.

"Please," she begged. She caught my hand as I put the truck in park. "I am willing to do *anything*." Her voice was breathless, full of promises. Honestly, everything about her was my type—except for the coercion. It left a bitter taste in my mouth, far stronger than even her being the messenger of Paco's demise. I'd been taken advantage of once and I'd be damned—even more damned—if I was ever going to 'own' anyone.

I pulled forty dollars out of my wallet. "Take this, and walk that direction for five miles." I pointed past her shoulder.

"And?"

"Don't come back."

Her face crumpled and she started to cry. "Maya will kill me." Fat tears rolled down her cheeks, taking her eyeliner with them.

"That's not my problem," I repeated.

Her lips pouted, no doubt holding back curses, as she snatched the twenties from my hand—then crumpled them up and threw them at my feet. "Screw you, Jack!" she said, storming from the truck. I swung out on my own side, watching her go, holding herself with her arms, head low with sorrow—with my vampiric senses, I could still hear her crying and taste the salt of her tears. She whirled around, hair whipping. "I'm going to die—because of your stupid pride!"

Her words hit my hardened heart like a rock. Would Maya really kill her? I wouldn't put it past her. Maya was kind of a bitch, and being trapped under Rosalie's thumb for a century or so hadn't done her any favors. Now that she was free, her taking out her frustration on any other Rosalie-associated targets seemed likely.

The girl, what'd she say her name was—Luna?—was already quarter of a block away. "Get back in the car," I muttered under my breath, halfway hoping she wouldn't hear. But she did, she stopped and looked back. "I haven't changed my mind. Just—stay here."

"For how long?"

"As long as it takes. Not sure." I recognized Mattie's truck in the parking lot—other artists would be arriving shortly, if they hadn't given up on Dark Ink entirely. I didn't want them to see her with me and make assumptions about how I'd been spending my time.

She swallowed and got back into the passenger seat with sullen silence—and I realized she hadn't taken her backpack with her when she'd left. I'd been played. I ran my hands through my hair—I'd deal with that later. For now—Dark Ink called.

KEEP READING
BLOOD AT DAWN: DARK INK TATTOO BOOK FIVE.

AND BE SURE TO JOIN CASSIE'S MAILING LIST FOR SECRET SCENES, MORE CHARACTER ART, MERCHANDISE, AND EXTRA STORIES!

# DARK INK TATTOO SERIES

Don't miss the rest of the Dark Ink Tattoo Series.

...with more to come!

# ALSO BY CASSIE ALEXANDER

Check out cassiealexander.com for content/trigger warnings.

**The Dark Ink Tattoo series**

Blood of the Pack

Blood at Dusk

Blood at Midnight

Blood at Moonlight

Blood at Dawn

Blood of the Dead *(January 2023)*

The Longest Night (Newsletter Bonus Story & Audio)

**Edie Spence Series**

Nightshifted

Moonshifted

Shapeshifted

Deadshifted

Bloodshifted

**Transformation Trilogy** *(Coming early 2023)*

Bend Her

Break Her

Make Her

**Standalone Stories**

AITA?

Her Ex-boyfriend's Werewolf Lover

Her Future Vampire Lover

The House

Rough Ghost Lover

## WRITTEN WITH KARA LOCKHARTE

### THE PRINCE OF THE OTHER WORLDS SERIES

Dragon Called

Dragon Destined

Dragon Fated

Dragon Mated

Dragons Don't Date (Prequel Short Story)

Bewitched (Newsletter Exclusive Bonus Story)

### THE WARDENS OF THE OTHER WORLDS SERIES

Dragon's Captive

Wolf's Princess

Wolf's Rogue *(Coming soon)*

Dragon's Flame *(Coming soon)*

# ABOUT THE AUTHOR

Cassie Alexander is a registered nurse and author. She's written numerous paranormal romances, sometimes with her friend Kara Lockharte. She lives in the Bay Area with one husband, two cats, and one million succulents.

Sign up for Cassie's mailing list here or go to cassiealexander.com/newsletter to get free books, bonus scenes, even more character art, and cat photos!

Printed in Great Britain
by Amazon